A Remnant Hope

Revival Well

Copyright © 2015 Revival Well Ministry

All rights reserved.

ISBN: **1515264505**
ISBN-13: **978-1515264507**

If you would like to contact the author, please email us at

revivalwellministry@gmail.com

www.RevivalWell.org

No part of this book may be reproduced, stored in a retrieval system, or transmitted by any means without the written permission of the Author.

Scripture taken from the HOLY BIBLE, NEW INTERNATIONAL VERSION ®. Copyright © 1973, 1978, 1984 by International Bible Society. Used by permission of Zondervan Publishing House. All Rights reserved.

The 'NIV' and 'New International Version' trademarks are registered in the United States Patent and Trademark Office by International Bible Society. Use of their trademark requires the permission of International Bible Society.

I'd like to thank my father Gordon for his hard work in editing this story which the Holy Spirit put on my heart. I would also like to thank my Father in Heaven who continues to be my inspiration every day

CONTENTS

	ACKNOWLEDGMENTS	I
	INTRODUCTION	PG 1
1	PEOPLE OF HOPE	PG 6
2	MORE PEOPLE OF HOPE	PG 28
3	A GROWING HOPE	PG 46
4	MYSTERY OF HOPE	PG 69
5	A FUTURE HOPE	PG 96
6	GATHERING HOPE	PG 115
7	HOPE REVEALED	PG 142
8	A DAY OF HOPE	PG 162
9	HOPE OVERCOMES	PG 186

There is surely a future hope for you, and your hope will not be cut off

Proverbs 23:18

INTRODUCTION

Soon after the Third World War a decision was taken worldwide to create a new order of society where all people would be regarded as global citizens. The war had been absolutely devastating to the Middle East and had its cause blamed directly upon the conflicts between the various religions in that region. It was in this context that the Global International Beliefs Organisation, or GIBO for short, was formed at the direct request of the United Nations. Their aim was to create a global religion with a *Global Basis of Faith*. The idea was not to outlaw all former religions but to amalgamate them all into the one faith. Once this was established, all religious organisations and groups were required to register with GIBO in order to be recognised as legitimate.

After a short changeover period, the activities of all illegitimate groups would be made illegal. As part of the registration process they had to sign an agreement to declare that their doctrines would be primarily set to comply with GIBO standards. Naturally, from the outset, this caused uproar across the globe but, when faced with the fact that it was religion that had led to the world's worst war, people could not successfully resist the new system for long.

Immediately following the introduction of the new system, it was possible for most governments to cross reference people's previous tax records with their GIBO registration details, as most of the religious organisations had previously registered themselves in order to claim tax exemption. Furthermore, many individuals in various countries could now be traced by the same procedure, as they had previously helped their organisations claim back tax by registering their own donations. This cross-referencing therefore helped governments to quickly identify and challenge any groups or individuals who had refused to register. The main religious groups were the first to yield under the weight of pressure and, as soon as they did, it helped GIBO gain credibility and domination worldwide. The *Global Basis of Faith* was soon introduced in schools and colleges and all public employees were required to sign their agreement to it.

One of the central aims of GIBO was to make sure that people everywhere accepted social diversity. Acceptance of people, in all walks of life in a non-judgemental way, was now the standard. The media presented this as a historic moment and the world's best ever attempt at tackling racism and prejudice. While some of the principles seemed good, at ground level it meant that churches, for instance, could no longer refuse to comply with particular demands by biblical reasoning. Homosexuals, for example, would now have to be allowed to get married in churches and even run those churches. This would be seen as progressive and the final solution for what the world had been moving towards for years.

Of course, in some countries the tracing of some religious groups proved to be difficult and governments often sent in armed police to arrest individuals or groups who were refusing to comply with the new system. As a result, there were battles fought in various places where there was resistance against the globalisation of religion. The outcome of this enforcement was the formation of a global armed force trained to defend GIBO using whatever means necessary.

Anyone who chose to live outside the new rules was automatically labelled a fanatic, a radical who should be considered dangerous and treated accordingly. The media would often show bombings to be the work of such fanatics, which reduced any such hope of the wider public supporting their cause. In reality the bombings were the work of the global armed forces. This type of coverage was considered by those in power to be a great way of tackling those in resistance. For example, if a school were found to be teaching 'fanatical' religious doctrines, then that school would be bombed and the fanatics blamed. Tackling rebellion in this underhanded secretive way hastened the process of conversion and, in fact, the secret became so big that no one would have dared to let it out. Individual people were also made examples of and there were frequent cases where, for example, pastors refusing to marry homosexuals were prosecuted and thrown into jail.

Where whole countries decided against supporting the new world system and refused to proscribe those who were labelled fanatics, the global armed forces attacked using an overwhelming show of strength. This army was very well equipped and drew support from most of the larger nations, so, resistance by any country was generally seen as madness. In fact it was suicidal. The first country to rebel was made an example of by GIBO. They detonated two nuclear bombs over the capital, killing multiple thousands of people, wiping out the government and leaving the country decimated and in chaos. Afterwards a puppet government was established, one which was submitted to the global order. Of course, the use of nuclear bombs was blamed upon the religious fanatics and the majority of people believed these news broadcasts. This event then set standards for defeating other rebellious nations and a shock-wave spread across the globe. Those still in resistance could see that there was no limit to the action that would be taken against them if they stood their ground.

For those who tried to stay true to their faith, many of them ended up being dragged unwillingly into violence and wars whereby they lost all sense of what they used to believe. They wanted peace but all that faced them was persecution and bloodshed.

In truth, God's enemy, Satan, had done his job well by causing attention to be focused in different ways on various religions. The Muslims, for example, were used by the Enemy as puppets to help accomplish his ultimate goal – to drag Israel into a disastrous war. With the Christians, however, his focus had been very different. His plan was to infiltrate as many church belief systems as possible and introduce or promote religiosity, empty worship and division. He loved it when churches focussed on being organised because by doing this they became more predictable and he would know when they would meet and for how long. He knew that the more religious that churches became, that more and more people in them would be kept at a distance from God. Church people like others, loved routine and so gladly fell into the trap of exchanging a true relationship with the living God for a program.

The Enemy also used false teachers to lure people to accept false beliefs such as if they merely recited a simple prayer and attended church services, they would get to heaven. This kind of religion became 'the Broad Road' that Jesus warned about in the Bible. In effect, the Enemy was just setting people up for what was to come and to make them submissive and dependent on their church leaders so that they would not object to their being signed up to the *Global Basis of Faith*. As a result, most churches got so caught up in being religious and in being linked to the world system that they were unable to make any resistance to GIBO and therefore they folded and most of their people submitted to the new order. They did not know the truth, or even how to listen to the truth. They only heard the voice of their church leaders, who were now encouraging them to comply with GIBO.

However, there were those who remained faithful, people whom God had prepared in advance for what was now happening. Most of these had wisely left their churches as they became tainted by the teachings of the new order. However, God saw these faithful believers as His people, the true church of God. They listened to Him above all others in authority. They obeyed Him first and not religion or church pastors. They were persecuted for their stance, but of course, at the same time, they were released into amazing experiences of God. They had personally discovered 'the Narrow Way'. They walked in it, trusting fully in God and in Him alone.

These righteous exiles also became social outcasts. They were no longer welcome anywhere and were persecuted, scorned and ridiculed for the truth that they spoke of. Their numbers dwindled but they cried out all the more to God to bring back hope and for God to reveal His glory once again.

CHAPTER 1

PEOPLE OF HOPE

Sarah looked worryingly at the head nurse but she showed no reaction whatsoever.

"He's coming," a voice was yelling, "he's coming to kill her!"

"You're going to have to get used to things like that," the head nurse said bluntly, seeing the concern on Sarah's face.

It was Monday and Sarah's first day in her new job. She had very little work experience before this and so she was feeling somewhat nervous. She had come on board as a carer to assist the nurses and so was a bit concerned about what the job might entail. The rising level of shouts coming from down the corridor weren't helping her nerves at all.

"Who is that down there?" she asked.

"Oh, just some homeless man that they have taken off the streets.

They'll stick him in a room for a day or two then probably let him out. We get all sorts here but don't worry, you will soon get the hang of it."

The head nurse stood up and led her out of the room and they walked down the corridor to where the voices were coming from. As they turned a corner, Sarah saw two of her colleagues manhandling a rugged looking man with a long beard and scruffy hair. She saw that he was wearing some sort of brown jacket with rips and tears all over it and even though they were still a couple of yards away, she could smell a pungent odour coming from him.

If that were me, I'd change my clothes and take a shower after being near him, she thought.

"Do you get a lot of homeless people around here?" she asked naively.

The head nurse shook her head.

Sarah had recently moved out of the city and was still quite new to this town where she had decided to settle. Job prospects had proved to be better here at the local hospital due to the psychiatric wards whereas back in the city she had only ever been offered part-time work which would not have been enough to support her. The hospital itself dated back to the time when they used to move patients suffering with TB out to the countryside to give them relief from their symptoms. That had been a long time ago. There had not been much of a town there before that which is maybe why it had been given the name 'Hope'. While she pondered this, she watched the other two carers get the man strapped down. She stood at the door and gave a half smile to the man who was still choosing to shout out at the top of his voice.

"He's coming! He's coming!"

"What do you think he is talking about?" she asked.

The head nurse turned to her and just raised her eyebrow. Sarah saw her expression and shut her mouth. The nurse stepped forward and gave the man a shot in the arm to sedate him. Then they all exited the room, the nurse turned and locked the door behind them. Sarah could hear the mumblings of the man fade away into a silence which seemed even spookier than the yelling that she had heard earlier.

It was not until Thursday that Sarah came into contact with the homeless man again. She had almost forgotten about him having discovered that to be employed at this hospital entailed long hours and hard work. In fact she was quite surprised to see him still there, especially after what the head nurse had said to her on her first night. But now here he was sitting peacefully on a chair by his bed looking calmly out the window. She glanced at his chart; the name read 'John Doe'.

She came over to him and bent down to his eye-level.

"So we still haven't found out who you are, have we?" she said softly.

He looked her in the eye briefly and saw that she had kindness in her heart. This made him warm up to her presence. He looked pleadingly at her and whispered softly,

"You have to get me out of here."

She put her hand on his arm.

"Of course, of course, let's just get you better first. Okay?"

"No, no, no," he said, speaking a little louder. "Time is running out and I need to be out there. I have to give the people an important message."

"Please keep calm," she said gently. "You don't want them, you know who, coming back," she added with a little twinkle in her eye.

Sarah may not have been at the hospital very long but already she had observed that at least two of the other carers treated people roughly. She had noted how the patients cowered in fear whenever they passed close by.

"Please help me. I know you will," he said, still looking at her imploringly.

"Would you like to watch a little TV?" she said tactfully in an attempt to change the subject.

He nodded.

She reached into the pocket of her tunic and took out a remote control. All of the carers carried them. They couldn't leave them in the rooms because some patient had once decided to injure himself with the batteries. Now all the TVs were controlled only by the staff.

"Anything you'd like to watch?" she asked as the screen lit up.

"The News, the News," he responded excitedly changing his position so that he could see the screen more clearly.

Immediately his eyes fastened on the TV.

Job done, she thought as she stayed for a while tidying up things in the room before moving on to see the next patient.

There was something about this man that made her curious.

She pondered, *why is he still here? Why isn't he receiving any treatment?*

She shrugged the thoughts out of her mind quickly as soon as she entered the next room and saw a floor covered in sick.

She sighed and thought to herself, *I don't see myself doing this for the rest of my life.*

Two hours later, after calls to several rooms, she popped back to see John. He was still glued to the TV fascinated by the news. As she watched, she noted how he wasn't just looking at the TV. His mouth was moving as if he was mumbling something quietly to himself. Sarah had seen plenty of homeless people back in the city, out on the streets with their paper cups asking people for spare change. She'd almost always passed by 'on the other side' but the words 'spare change' had always reached her ears. They always looked so hopeless but she knew better than most about the drug-taking that went with homelessness. She could see the effect of it in their faces.

But this guy, he's different; he shows no signs at all of drug taking. He is different!

Suddenly John stopped gazing at the TV. He looked down and started to breathe very deeply.

"John, are you ok?" she asked quickly.

He stood up and turned to look at her. His eyes had changed. She had never seen such determination in all her life. She took a step backwards in fear not knowing what he might do next. He did not move forward though. They just stood there, captured in a gaze. Then he spoke with a strong and powerful voice, much stronger than it was earlier.

"A flight broken in the night," he said, "wings lost in the waves. Depths they search but shallow they lay, all in flame except Luke. Luke, a deal he made, the witness shot was not the one they need, and so he comes to kill her, the descendant of Artie Stevens."

As soon as he finished speaking he collapsed to his knees shaking all over for a minute or two. Sarah knelt down beside him while at the same time calling for help. As her hand touched his arm, she noticed that every pore on his skin seemed to have come to life. Goose bumps covered his body briefly, and then faded.

Soon, other staff rushed into the room and helped her get John back into his bed. She switched off the TV and sighed as she thought about the effect it had on him.

That's the last time that I'll put that on for him.

However the experience left her shaken and, even later as she finished her shift, she couldn't stop thinking about it. She left the hospital which was just off the main street and walked towards her apartment. It was only a couple of minutes walk. She was so much more content to live here in this small town after her experiences in the big city. This was probably because she had originally grown up in a small country town, although she hardly ever went back there since her parents had died a few years back.

They had left her enough money to get a start in life and she had been able to pay off a large portion of the purchase price of the apartment in which she now lived. She knew that she wouldn't want to stay there indefinitely as she wanted to one day settle down and have children.

Perhaps even with Steve, she thought.

Steve was her on-off boyfriend since coming to town. They had met the very first day that she had come to have an interview at the hospital. She had stayed in town for a couple of days to look at potential homes. They met randomly in a local bar and had hit it off straight away. That was over a month ago. Since then, they had been living a life of sin but she was hoping that the fun side would get more serious at some point.

But it's still early yet, she thought as she walked up the stairs and entered her apartment.

It was already late at night.

Those 12-hour shifts are a killer, she thought as she plonked herself down on the sofa with her micro-waved TV dinner.

Four hours later she awoke. The TV was still blaring at full volume. Her tray and dinner dishes were on the coffee table in front of her. She glanced at the clock that was on the other side of the room, it was just after 3am and she rebuked herself for not having taken herself to bed to sleep properly rather than dozing on the sofa. She stood up and was just about to switch off the TV when some words caught her attention.

The newsreader was saying, "Breaking news, Flight AJ5935 has been reported missing and is thought to have gone down somewhere over the Atlantic Ocean. The famous musician, Luke Tyrell, is thought to have been on board. Radio contact was lost around 11 pm and there had been no contact since that time. Air and Sea Rescue services on both sides of the Atlantic are organising a major search starting with the last known location of the plane. Terrorism has not been ruled out at this point."

Sarah sat down with shock, staring at the screen.

"That's impossible!" she said, her voice a mere whisper.

Jenny screamed.

"Harold, Harold it's your turn!" prompted Suzie, shaking her husband awake.

"Huh," he huffed as he stirred from his sleep.

He could already hear the sobs coming from the adjoining bedroom.

"Again!" he protested.

He sat up and put on his slippers.

"This is not normal," he said, "it really isn't."

"What would you expect when..." Suzie's voice faded.

"Yea, I know," he said, understanding what his wife was referring to.

"COMING Jenny," he called, getting up and stumbling towards the door.

Walking slowly, he noted that, according to the clock on the wall, it had just gone three in the morning. He opened the bedroom door and walked out into the corridor. Walking straight into Jenny's bedroom, he saw her sitting up in bed with her teddy clutched in her arms, she was rubbing her eyes and crying loudly and his heart moved with pity for her. He sat down on the bed beside her and wrapped her in his arms.

"What happened Jenny?" he asked, "why are you crying?"

"Bad man, bad man!" she sobbed, repeating the words over and over.

"It's okay Jenny, its okay," he spoke softly to her.

"It was only a dream. See, you're here in your own bedroom, in your own bed."

She stopped crying and began to look around.

"There is no bad man here, see," he reassured her.

She nodded, not quite convinced.

"Now Jenny, it's still very early in the morning. You need to lie down and go back to sleep," he said as he stood up.

He couldn't help but feel sorry for Jenny as he tucked her back under her covers. She had been through a lot but, in truth, he knew that there was nothing much that he and Suzie could do. Her life had been traumatised, maybe forever and he feared that it just might be so.

He returned to his bedroom and found that Suzie had gone back to sleep so he lay back down as quietly as he could. Lying there awake, he thought back to when they had discussed the upheaval that a child might cause to their lives. In fact, lack of sleep was something that they had prepared for but that had been in expectation of adopting a new-born baby. Instead, they had adopted Jenny, a four-year old who had suffered serious trauma. Only weeks previous to the adoption, she had been found next to her dead parents, fully awake and crying, covered in the their blood. Not even the police had any idea what the little girl had been through during the last moments of her parents' lives; they could only speculate. In fact, the whole thing had been a huge mystery. The police had never done much by way of an investigation of the murder. Instead, they described it simply as a break-in that went wrong and they had quickly moved to find Jenny a new home. Harold and Suzie had learned about Jenny's sad history from the lady in the adoption agency who had dealt with her case. Harold was glad of one thing though. He was happy that Jenny hadn't ended up in the state care-system. He had been through that system and so he knew from his own experience that it would not have done her any good.

Now weeks after the adoption, it had begun to happen as regularly as clockwork. Every night, at least once, Jenny would wake up after having a nightmare. Sometimes he had felt so sorry for her that he had even tried to pray and ask God to take away her painful memories. It was strange for him to do that as he didn't really believe in God. It had simply been an idea that sprang from the mercy in his heart. Suzie, of course, didn't like to talk about the 'event' as she called it. She always put it off and changed the subject as if to pretend that no such thing had ever happened. Whether or not they ignored the cause, they would not be able to ignore the regular broken sleep. During the daytime, Jenny was also very reserved, shy and quiet. She would often stare into space or even avoid social contact altogether. Jenny had a broken heart and they both knew it. Although she responded well to their love and attention, the truth was that life with Jenny was difficult. Harold had already used up most of his annual holidays to help deal with the changes in their home. He would not be able to take any more time off, not if he still wanted to have a break at Christmas.

Despite everything, over the last month Harold had come to love Jenny and he held a special place in his heart for her. He was beginning to feel like a real dad.

He drifted in and out of sleep for a while as he lay beside his wife but eventually at seven he decided to rise and get Jenny her breakfast. This allowed Suzie to have an extra hour in bed but, at eight, he had to leave for work and so he woke his wife with a gentle kiss on her cheek.

Both Harold and Suzie were a middle-aged and in their forties. He was starting to grey on top but both of them were still full of life, all except the life that would enable them to have children of their own. They had always loved each other, even from childhood, and always knew that they would grow old together. It had not always been easy, especially in their twenties when they discovered that they would never be able to have children by natural means. This was something which affected them both differently. He took up fishing, and would go once a week, usually on a Saturday, to get some space. His wife, on the other hand, had started socialising a lot more with her friends. Both of these pastimes had lasted ever since then, that is until Jenny arrived. She may have been traumatised, but Jenny was still a little 'bundle of joy' to them, something they had wanted for many years and now had the opportunity to keep. It was a miracle. At the front door he kissed them both goodbye and headed off to work.

Harold led a simple life. He worked for a local legal firm, the only one in their town. In actual fact, they were the only lawyers in the whole area including the surrounding towns, and so his work kept him really busy. He had originally started out as an auctioneer but had gradually drifted into helping people with various legal problems. Eventually he had gone back to college to study law at night.

It was nearly lunch time when Suzie called him. She sounded quite upset on the phone as she told him something about Jenny and about the TV. Feeling anxious, he had a quick word with his boss, who said that seeing as though it was Friday Harold could take an early lunch and call by his house. What greeted him there was nothing he could have ever expected. He stood at the kitchen door, his wife was seated on the sofa and Jenny was smiling and singing and hopping around the room in some sort of dance.

"What the...?" he started.

"I know! Right!" retorted his wife, cutting him off.

"What's happening? What's going on?" he asked as he watched Jenny's antics.

"I sat down after ironing and was flicking through the channels on the TV to see what was on. Then the phone rang and I went out to the kitchen to answer it and I left her here. I was only on the call for a few minutes; it was Val saying that he might come down next week on Monday evening.

Anyway, when I came back into the room, she was behaving like this and she's been doing it for over an hour now. I don't know what's come over her."

Harold was astounded and even more so considering that the TV had long since been switched off. Yet Jenny was still singing songs that neither of them had ever heard before. Since he had left the house, Jenny had changed from being a social recluse into the happiest little girl Harold had ever set eyes upon.

"What is she singing about?" he asked Suzie.

"I think that the channel that I had left on when I left the room was one of those pirate Christian TV channels that you hate. I think she is singing about Jesus."

Harold listened carefully to Jenny's words and soon enough he heard her say 'Jesus'.

"That's totally weird," he said scratching his head. "Where has she got all of this from? It couldn't have been from just watching the TV."

His wife agreed, nodding her head.

"Maybe her, parents, were Christian fanatics or something?" she whispered.

"That would explain a lot," he stated, careful not to say too much in front of Jenny.

"Err, I'd best grab something to eat while I'm here," he said, noticing the time.

"You sit down; I'll make you something," said Suzie.

He sat down and leaned back on his chair watching young Jenny bounce around the room like a kangaroo, singing about Jesus. He would have laughed if he wasn't aware of what it could mean both for her and for them. Harold couldn't remember exactly when the government had changed the laws relating to religious practice but he knew that things that were out-of-the-ordinary were frowned upon. He remembered how he had felt about it at the time, fully supporting the idea of getting rid of religious social discrimination. Although in some ways he had questioned whether it would work as previous times in history, such as the Prohibition, abolition had not worked but forced activities to continue underground.

Harold had an anxious thought. *What if our Jenny had belonged to one of these strange fanatic groups?* He thought long and hard about it until his wife came in with some food for them.

"Jenny come and sit down to eat," he said.

She came obediently and sat on the carpet next to the coffee table.

A cold sweat broke out across Harold's head. He shared a mutual glance with his wife as little Jenny bowed her head and said, "Thank you, Lord, for all that you have given us today."

Mr Balding, in spite of what his name suggested, actually had a full head of hair but the years had long since passed since he used to dye it. Now, his hair had become pure silver, a feature which showed his age.

"Ah, Balding, good to see you," beamed the police commissioner as they shook hands, "sit down, sit down."

"Thanks," said Mr Balding and taking the direction, sat on the chair provided.

"How many years has it been? Three?" asked the police commissioner, trying to recall how long it had been since Mr Balding left office.

"Six!" replied Mr Balding.

He had kept count of the years of his somewhat dull retirement. His wife had passed away several years before and their children were grown up and had families of their own.

"How are your children? Jonathan and Elisha, that right, isn't it?" asked the commissioner.

"Yes, they're good," replied Mr Balding, "Jonathan is over in France working in robotics and Elisha just got married and is now living in Glasgow," he added with a touch of pride and fond memories of his children.

"Did you go over for the wedding?"

"Oh, yeah! It was a great trip. Rained on the wedding day, though, but then what can you do about that?"

"One thing you can't stop in life is the weather," said the commissioner, nodding in agreement.

Then he pushed his chair back so that he could open the bottom drawer of his desk, and pulled out a brown coloured folder. Standing up, he went over to the internal office windows and pulled down all the blinds. Balding knew immediately that this was a signal that something secret was about to be discussed.

"I guess you're wondering why I asked you to come," said the commissioner as he caught Mr Balding's glance at what he was holding.

"Something to do with that folder which you're holding?" he inquired.

The commissioner gave a sigh as he sat back down.

"A lot has changed since you left," he said, "all these new laws! They are impossible to police and the politicians are always putting pressure on us to enforce them."

Mr Balding sensed what might be coming.

"I was hoping that we might be able to hire your services. I figured you might appreciate the extra money too. You see, I need someone that I can trust for this, someone who is not connected to all the usual day-to-day stuff here at the station."

"To do what?" asked Balding, needing more information.

"A bit of undercover work," explained the commissioner.

Balding began to shake his head. He was taken aback by what the commissioner had said and immediately considered putting his jacket back on to leave.

"Why not just send in one of the young guys? They're always eager," he argued.

"The truth is, I already have but they get spotted a mile away by this group that we're interested in. I'm not sure how they do it but they do. Let's be honest. You're not really a policeman anymore, just ..."

"An old man?" Balding interjected.

"Yes, you get my drift," said the commissioner.

"Who is this group then? What are they about?" asked Balding, his curiosity growing.

The commissioner tapped the brown coloured folder.

"All the details of what we know are right here," he said. "They are religious fanatics and are suspected of having committed acts of terrorism and fanaticism over the years. We just haven't been able to pin them down and so we basically need someone to infiltrate them, to find out when and where they meet, to find out their real identities and where they live. You know, the usual reconnaissance stuff."

"And what do you want to achieve?" enquired Balding wandering where all this would lead.

"To make arrests and bring these people to trial. To get all of them would be preferable but if it's just one or two then that will have to suffice," replied the commissioner. From his expression, Balding could see that he really wanted a successful outcome, and soon.

"Will I have to wear wires? Get video?" asked Balding, imagining himself as a professional spy.

"No, none of that. When you read the files you'll realise that these people are already being monitored to a degree. Their emails are monitored as well as other communication online. They have been even captured on cameras in locations where they are known to congregate from time to time."

Balding thought this over for a moment.

"Then I am guessing that this is a hush-hush job," he said. "So nobody except you will know that I'm working undercover! Right? So what assurances do I have that I won't become entangled in the mess and find myself getting arrested?"

"Here," the commissioner said, handing him a bundle of papers stapled together.

"It's a contract that specifies what exactly you're doing for us and includes a letter ensuring that neither you nor your family will be prosecuted for breach of laws concerning religious fanaticism, or anything of that nature. On page four you'll see the amount payable through the contract. That sum of money will be paid anonymously into your account on a weekly basis."

Mr Balding did a quick scan of the documents.

"I see that you have a lot of stuff covered. What makes you think that I'll take the chance though, that I'll take the risks?"

"Did I ever tell you about my dad?" asked the commissioner.

Balding shook his head.

"He was a cop too. He worked the beat his whole working life. I remember after his retirement that he was always restless, always wanting to do more. I guess you could say he was bored. I kinda figured you might like one last piece of excitement."

There was a long pause. Silence pervaded the room. Balding reckoned that the commissioner himself must not be far from retirement. Then it dawned on him. It was he who was bored, stuck in his office. This affair was going to give him that piece of excitement he had referred to.

At last, he gave his reply, "If it's alright with you, I'll think it over," he said.

"Good! Good! Take all the time you need. Read the files but take this with you now. It's a phone that makes calls that can't be traced, the latest technology. It makes it almost impossible for anyone to hack in and listen in to your calls and its location and ownership are completely untraceable."

Mr Balding looked the phone over. He didn't much like mobile phones but he had to admit this really did look the part.

"My stealth-phone," he said to himself.

"Call me only from that phone," said the commissioner, "I've put my numbers in there for you." Then he added proudly, "The phone also has a built-in emergency transmitter. On the main screen, simply tap the alert icon and it will send a message out on police radio to send back-up to your GPS location."

"That's nifty alright," said Balding looking the phone over again.

He stood up and slid the phone into his pocket. He then stuffed the folder inside his trouser belt and fastened his jacket.

The commissioner opened the blinds and then the door. They parted quietly so that no one in the outer office would take any note of Balding as he passed by.

As soon as Balding reached home, he sat down with a cup of coffee and started to scan through the files. At first he found it difficult. There was a lot of content and it had been a long time since he had done this kind of work. He noticed their speech in emails was written by using some sort of code. There were sentences that seemed out of place and didn't make sense.

I wonder if I could break their code, he thought. *Maybe, I can learn it if I get close enough.*

What really surprised him was that the locations of their recorded meetings were in several smaller towns and also even in the city.

They seem random, he thought, *they will be hard to track down.*

As he read on, he discovered that on three occasions meetings had been captured partially by a camera installed at a suspected location.

Three times. That's better odds than the other places.

He looked and frowned as he read the name of the town.

"Hope! I don't think I've ever heard of it," he said as he got up and walked over to his bookshelves to get out a map of the country so he could look it up.

"Hope! Now, where is Hope?" he said to himself as he began to examine the map index.

Linda fell down on to her bed. She could not get back up even if she had wanted to. It felt as if every muscle in her body ached. It had not been an easy week. One after the other, each of her three sons had been sick with a stomach bug leaving Linda on the go almost nonstop for the past seventy-two hours. Even now, as she lay there, she had no idea which of them would call out in need of her help. What she feared most of all right at this moment was for her to catch whatever it was the children had.

What would I do then? she thought.

She was just about to fall into a deep sleep when she felt her phone vibrating in her pocket.

Having deliberated whether to answer it or not, she finally reached for it and looked at the name on the screen. Such was her exhaustion, she had to concentrate for a moment before she realised who the caller was. It was her partner, Sam.

"Hi," she yawned, after she located the call button.

"Hey, where have you been all this time?" asked Sam in a somewhat aggressive tone.

"Don't start," she said with a tone in her voice that matched his.

"What do you mean 'don't start'? I haven't been able to get hold of you since Monday, and its Friday now!"

"The children have been sick."

"Oh, so when the children are sick you just ignore me, is that it? You could have at least texted me or something," he said, still angry.

"Listen Sam, I have been up to my eyes in sick and diapers. What do you expect me to do? Answer your beck and call as well?"

"Don't be stupid, Linda! Are you telling me that you had no time at all even to send a short text?"

"Nope," she answered, still matching his aggressive tone.

Sam paused for a moment, and Linda could hear him taking deep breaths.

Then he continued.

"I am over here fighting for our country and at the same time I'm earning a living to support you and the children. Then, when I want to say 'hi' to them, I just get the cold shoulder. That's not right, Linda! Are the children there, I want to say hello to them."

"They're sleeping," she replied, trying hard not to yawn again.

He was adamant that he wanted to talk to them.

"Can't you go and wake them up?" he demanded.

His demand made Linda see red. She sat up in the bed and raised her voice to make sure he heard every word clearly.

"They're SICK, Sam! What part of 'sick' do you not understand? And by the way, I never asked you to go over there to fight leaving me here to take care of everything while you're off gallivanting around God-knows-where."

The phone went dead.

Huh! Couldn't take the truth, she thought as she put the phone back into her pocket.

The battles between them had recently become a lot more regular. Sam was nearing the end of his current six-month tour of duty on the front line but nevertheless it was always like this when he was nearing the end of his tour. He always got more and more irritable, not that they didn't have arguments when he was at home. Whatever this row was about, what was going on between them was not what she had wanted when they had first moved in together.

Early on Saturday morning, when Linda woke, she found several voice messages on her phone. They were all from Sam apologising and asking after the children.

I'll let him stew for a while, she thought.

She was pleased to find that her oldest eldest boy had already come downstairs and, judging by the mess he had left in the kitchen, she could tell he had helped himself to breakfast.

"Feeling better now, George?" she asked.

He was sitting in the lounge watching the TV. He nodded.

That's good, she thought, *today is going to be easier.*

Then, on the spur of the moment, she said to him, "What do you say if we get your dad on Skype tonight?"

"Ok, mum," he said with a sniff.

She made herself a cup of tea and then poured some cornflakes into a bowl to get a boost before the other two stirred. It felt good to eat. Her normal routine had broken down due to all that had been going on. As the children hadn't been eating normal meals, she had not been eating proper meals herself either. Thinking about food, she remembered that she could really do with going to the store to get some groceries.

It will be a nightmare, she thought.

"Mum!" she heard a voice calling her from upstairs.

She reacted immediately and went upstairs to see which one of the children had called.

She went into the twin bedroom where the two youngest boys Jason and Damon slept but Jason wasn't there.

He must be in the bathroom.

Damon was in his cot. He was standing up and his sleep-suit was covered in vomit and she could smell even from where she stood that he urgently needed a diaper change.

"Mum!" the voice called again, from the bathroom.

Lifting Damon from his cot, Linda went into the bathroom. She placed Damon on the baby changer and helped Jason clean himself.

This done and Damon changed, she went back downstairs and let the boys watch TV. She went to finish her breakfast but found she was no longer in the mood to eat it.

"Jason, do you want anything to eat?" she asked.

He shook his head.

She decided to try and feed Damon and to get a drink for Jason.

He has to keep his fluids up.

After a few hours looking after the boys, Linda managed to take a quick shower. Then she got the boys ready to take a trip to the store but she had to change Damon another three times before even getting out the door. With Jason and Damon in the double-buggy and with George holding on at the side, she walked down out of her estate towards the main street. There was only one grocery store in Hope and its opening hours weren't very people-friendly, especially if you worked a 9-to-5 job but, Linda would have plenty of time to get what she needed before they closed. She hoped and prayed that her boys would be okay until she got back home.

Walking down the road, she realised that it felt good to be out of the house.

Maybe the fresh air will do us all some good, she thought.

"Morning!" said the storekeeper, smiling as she entered the store.

"Good morning," she replied. She had never bothered to learn the owner's name.

She pulled out the shopping list from her pocket and got busy looking around the store for everything on it. As she found each item, she placed it in her shopping basket that was balanced on top of the buggy.

At the dairy aisle, Linda left the buggy and the children behind in order to grab various items off the shelves. When she turned around she was surprised to see a young girl standing by the buggy talking to the children, especially to Jason. As Linda walked back, the little girl ran around the corner into another aisle. Linda followed after her to find out who she was and where she had gone but as she turned the corner she saw that the girl had actually run all the way to the checkouts where a lady reached out and took her by the hand.

She must have got away from her mum. I wonder who they are.

The mother's face seemed familiar to Linda but she was certain that she had never set eyes on the little girl before.

"Mommy!"

Linda heard Jason call her. She turned and went back to where she had left him and the other two children.

"Mommy!"

"Yes," she said bending down to him, "did you make a new friend?"

She noticed that as she was talking to him, Jason was struggling in his seat as if trying to get out.

"Jason, don't get out. You're not well!"

"No, mommy, I'm all better now," he announced.

"What do you mean you're all better?" asked Linda, totally taken aback by his answer.

"My ouch all gone," he said in his childish way.

Linda was astounded. She proceeded to lift him out of his buggy and, sure enough, he started running up and down the aisle. He hadn't been like this in days.

Then she looked at Damon. He looked remarkably better too; he was smiling and playing happily with one of his toys.

Okay, that's just weird!

She didn't know what to say but then she remembered the little girl who had been talking to them.

"Jason, come here," she called.

He ran back to her.

"What did the little girl say to you?" she enquired.

"It's a secret, Mommy. But now I am all better. See!"

As she reached the next aisle, Jason suddenly asked, "Can I have this?" pointing to a bar of chocolate on a display stand.

"Better is right!" said Linda aloud.

She snatched him away from the chocolate and headed straight for the checkout.

CHAPTER 2

MORE PEOPLE OF HOPE

Mr Smith was awakened by the sound of his alarm clock. He turned on his side and pressed the snooze button; it was no use. He was already awake and could feel his head pounding. The expected hangover from his Friday night was here. He rolled over but it just brought a reminder that she was not there beside him. Thinking about her made him angry. For months, on and off, she had been coming round to his place for some 'company' and would usually stay for breakfast too. It was certainly a time in his life which he would never boast about. It didn't matter so much that Lisa was gorgeous or that she had a keen mind and a good heart. It didn't matter because she was the wife of his boss, the very man he had worked under for years.

The whole affair had all started out quite innocently. He had been asked to attend the annual political conference which that year had been held in Las Vegas. Senator Holloway, his boss, had recently been caught up in a scandal. Smith vividly remembered the incident and the details of how the story broke. A school-child at a school in the senator's home town had been arrested by the police for practicing fanaticism. Not only that, but the child was the best friend of the senator's son. Unfortunately, the story had come out just before the conference and the media were hot on the senator's heels so he had extra meetings beyond the planned conference schedule to handle the situation, to meet with his political advisors, hold press conferences and issue press statements.

Smith had managed to avoid attending most of those extra meetings and took some personal time to enjoy the night life of Las Vegas. Then, one night, while he sat at the hotel bar, Lisa walked in. She was young, only twenty seven, as he discovered, the senator's third wife even though she was only half his age. Smith had always thought that she was good-looking but that night she walked in wearing a tight red dress, it caused him to feel attracted to her in a way that he had never felt before.

Why did I even talk to her? he thought to himself. Thinking back over recent events and shaking his head.

That night, Lisa had come over and sat down next to him. He was a friendly face as they had often passed by each other at the office, and she was bored because he husband had been so busy. Being about the same age, they hit it off almost instantly. It took him by surprise that she openly criticised the senator, saying that she had long suspected him of having affairs behind her back. This encouraged him to list the negative things that he had noticed himself about his boss. As they talked, they found more and more things that they had in common. They discovered, for instance, that Lisa had once lived in a town near to where he was from, although it had only been for a few months when she was a young child. Nevertheless, there was an instant bond between them.

After several drinks, they became quite tipsy and Lisa finally admitted that he could out-drink her and that she'd have to call it a night. That was the point that Smith could identify as being the point of bad decision, the point of no return. He had also decided to head up to his room and so they found themselves sharing the same elevator. He couldn't quite remember who kissed who first, but they definitely kissed. It was nothing more, nothing less. However, over the coming weeks they continued to grow closer and closer until, eventually, they were having a full blown affair.

After a while, Smith started to hope and dream that Lisa would leave the senator and come to live with him. In many ways, he was naïve and couldn't see the 'man-eater' streak that was in her. Before the senator, she had many-a-time broken hearts of anyone she wanted to, without a care. However, at first they were happy, especially when the senator was away and they could spend time together. At other times, though, it was torture having to pass by each other during working hours at the office refraining from showing any interest beyond a casual friendship. Senator Holloway, after all, was a powerful man; he could ruin Smith if he so chose.

The whole thing started to go downhill when Smith said to Lisa that he was falling in love with her. Even though she responded at first by expressing her mutual love for him, afterwards her attitudes began to change. Feelings of guilt started to manifest themselves and they caused tension between the two of them. They had no fights as such, but he could feel her gradually holding back from their previous love. He tried to overcome this and as she held back he would try to get closer to her. This began to 'freak' her out and her visits became less and less frequent. It was the same at work, no smile, not even a glance. He was boiling mad inside, ready to blow. Then it had all came to a head the night before.

As usual, after work on Friday the office staff had all gone out for drinks. The senator had left early but Lisa had stayed on and when Smith saw this, he hoped that she might rekindle her love for him. He approached her as she was coming back from the bathroom but she refused to talk to him. Following her rejection he started to drink, downing whiskey after whiskey but the more he drank the more enraged he became. As he lay there on his bed thinking about this, he still felt that same anger and frustration pulsing through his veins. However, he could not remember much more than that. Flashes of memories popped into his mind but not so much that he could list his actions after that point.

Just then, his phone started to vibrate on the bedside cabinet. He normally left it there and must have somehow have kept that routine despite arriving home in a drunken state the night before.

"Hello," he answered, finding it hard to speak without showing his resentment.

The voice said, "Finally! I've been trying to call you all morning!"

The words were spoken with anger. It was Lisa.

"What do you want?" he demanded.

"Smith," she said, "don't you remember what happened last night?"

"Not completely," he answered, wondering what she was going to say next.

"Let me tell you. You went and told everybody at the office party that you and I are... having an affair."

She started to sob but Smith doubted her tears were genuine.

She continued, "What am I going to do when my husband finds out?"

You'll deserve what you get, he thought to himself, though wisely not speaking the words.

"I'll lose everything, thanks to you and your big mouth. Why did you have to go and say all that? Why couldn't you just accept that it was over between us? Now you've got both of us into a big mess. Just you wait till my husband gets a hold of you."

She spoke angrily again but Smith's head was pounding too much for him to contemplate the possible implications of what she was saying.

He paused for a moment before answering.

"I don't care what happens to you," he said cruelly.

It was a blatant lie because in reality he did still care but he wasn't going to admit it to this 'man-eater' of a woman who had trampled all over his heart.

Linda returned once again to her sobbing.

"It's that fellow, Vincent," she said, her sobbing growing louder. "He's my husband's little pet and will go running to him. I know it. My husband probably already knows all about it."

She's right on that one, Smith thought.

He replied, "Look it's done now; there's nothing we can do to change things. Both of us are going to have to face the consequences of what went on between us."

Lisa continued as if she hadn't heard a word of what he had said.

"Maybe you could call him and say that you were drunk and that you made it all up!"

"Lisa," said Smith, "he'll take one look at your face and know you're lying. He isn't stupid, you know! You don't need to worry too much though. Just dangle a few of the affairs that he has had in front of his nose. Maybe you can make him come crawling back to you instead."

At this Lisa stopped and went quiet.

"I'm going now," he said off-heartedly, "I need coffee."

"Fine then, I won't bother you again," she muttered.

"Good!"

He checked that the call had ended and replaced his phone on the cabinet. He was alone again in the quietness. He decided to forget coffee for now and instead try to get more sleep. He was just about to lie down but his phone started to ring again.

"Hello?" he answered, more guardedly this time.

"Smith? Hi, it's Vincent," said the voice.

That backstabber, thought Smith.

Vincent continued, "Listen, there has been fallout following what went on last night and, as you know, my job as chief of staff for the senator is to take care of delicate matters such as this."

Smith recalled how Vincent had once handled the case of a 17 year old girl who had to be hushed up after spending a night with the senator.

They won't touch me, he thought, *I know too much.*

Vincent continued, "Our main concern is that the media might get wind of this. We've discussed it here and we think it would be best that you take leave of absence for a while. The senator feels quite strongly about it."

"So he knows!" gasped Smith, "already?"

"He has known about it from the very start. Now we want it to just go away. So Smith, take a few weeks off, we'll be in contact soon. By the way, it would be best if you stayed clear of Lisa too."

"That won't be a problem," said Smith.

"Good," said Vincent curtly.

Smith guessed that Vincent was more than likely with the senator as he was talking and so he quickly said goodbye and hung up.

Then, remembering what Vincent had just said, he moaned, "Ugh! Leave? I hate leave!"

Then he rolled over on his side and considered his options. Where could he disappear to? He could think of only one place, his home town, Hope.

Pastor Edgeworth's drove his black SUV through town and went on out to the lane that led to the lake and his driveway. As he entered it he passed large black wrought-iron gates which marked the start of a long avenue leading towards his summer-house. The pastor had been coming here every year when on sabbatical leave ever since he bought the property fifteen years earlier, soon after becoming senior pastor of Greywood International Church in California. His predecessor had emphasised the importance of taking time away from the congregation in order to focus on getting more in touch with God. That was where it all began. But now, he found that his job as senior pastor was so stressful for him, with people, one after another, always complaining about this or that or coming to talk about their problems. It seemed as if his phone was ringing by day and by night.

Whenever he got to his summer-house in Hope he would relax, put his feet up, switch off his phone, have a bit of fun, or go for a swim in the pool. The four weeks he spent there every year would go by very quickly, and the return trip was always filled with dread as he headed back to the congregation that drained his energy.

He stepped out of the SUV and strolled through the arched doorway into the house. Although he called it a house, in reality it was more of a mansion. It had twelve bedrooms, nine bathrooms, two kitchens and several reception rooms. As well as that, they had a swimming pool, a sauna, a tennis court and six acres of land right next to the nature reserve that surrounded the lake. One could walk out with ease across the garden and over to the lakeside. For security he had put a twenty-four hour alarm system in place with fences to protect his property on each side. The only exception was the side facing the lake because that was what he loved most about his 'sabbatical home', the amazing view. The system monitored movement within the grounds and the mansion had many security cameras both inside and out, so the access from the lake was still monitored.

He found his wife Gloria in the kitchen, putting flowers into vases.

"Hi, darling," he said graciously.

"Hi," she said, greeting him with a sideways hug.

"How was the trip down?" she asked.

They never travelled together. She would normally spend a few extra weeks here without him.

"Fine, fine," he answered.

"How are things here?"

"Good, yes! I picked these this morning. Aren't they lovely? I'll unpack your stuff in a while if you want to leave them here for the time being."

"Sure, okay," the pastor said, happy to leave his suitcases by the door.

From there he walked down the hall to his study, taking just his briefcase with him.

This will be a long trip if Gloria's going to be hanging around like this, he thought.

Their marriage was a farce and he knew it. He had tried once to talk to her about it, to get her to face the truth that there was nothing between them anymore but she didn't want to know and she certainly didn't want a divorce. She had come from an upper class family in England and getting divorced was still frowned upon by them.

He opened his briefcase, took out his laptop and placed it on his desk.

As he sat down, his thoughts drifted back to the night before. He had actually been cuddled up on his sofa with a young widow from the church named Sandra. Her husband had died in the war and she had come to him seeking comfort. She was quite an attractive young woman and he had fancied her straightaway but then things had gone a bit too far. It didn't bother him that he was being unfaithful. He justified it because he knew that his wife no longer loved him that way anymore. Sandra was a very caring person and her presence was like a breath of fresh air to him.

"Do you really have to go?" she had pleaded whilst cuddled up beside him.

"I always go," he answered, "not going would make people suspicious."

"I don't care," she said.

He frowned at her.

"You could take me with you," she prompted.

"You know I can't," he retorted.

Looking back, he could still see the look of disappointment on her face.

In all honesty, he wanted to keep his distance from her. Things had become a bit blurred and he needed the relationship to cool down. He knew that if it ever got out what had been going on between them, he would lose his job, his income too. He didn't want that, especially his income.

"I have a plan," he muttered to himself.

He turned on his laptop. It was top-of-the-range model, and one of the latest models. It had loads of memory and had that pre-installed instant-on software which he always found handy. Within moments, he had logged into his online banking service and was looking over his transactions for the past month. The church income had increased over the years because he knew how to do his job well. He always taught in a way that encouraged people. He invariably told nice stories and people soaked up every word of his sermons. Usually, he would have people coming up to him after the services telling him how much his sermons had blessed them. This of course would have been impossible if it weren't for several 'pillars of the church', as he called them. These were a group of dedicated volunteers who gave their time and energy in order to support him in everything, from the running of the choir to the paying of the electricity bills.

The church itself was situated in a well-to-do area and so the majority of the people who attended were quite rich and also willing to give their money to a good cause. This suited the pastor fine. Years before, they had proceeded with a re-development in order to enlarge their building and this had all been paid for without taking out any loans thanks to the generous donations given by the congregation. The weekly donations had continued to increase then due to the bigger seating capacity and increased attendance. Then he organised book sales and several fundraising events alongside the other main church activities, all in order to get an even greater income. He smiled as he saw that the balance in his secret personal savings account had now reached almost three million dollars. This amount was separate from his other savings which were mainly the result of run-of-the-mill stuff. In this particular account, however, he had hidden all the little extras. He had actually begun saving money like this right from the time he took up his position as senior pastor. Now it was also his fail-safe plan in case Gloria did finally decide to divorce him. He was certain that she would never find out about his money. Nobody knew about it. It was his secret and also his secret joy as he logged into the account on a daily basis to look it over and to transfer money into it from elsewhere.

Finished with the banking, he logged out of the account and opened his email. There were two emails from Sandra.

I'll read them later, he said to himself as he switched his computer off.

He walked across the room and pulled out a study Bible from the bookshelf and also a few reference books that he liked to use and placed them down on his desk. Before coming, he had been teaching through Romans but he had now completed the book. He knew that he would need to have a new set of sermons ready for his return following his sabbatical leave. The church people would always anticipate his return which coincided with the first term of the new school term. They wanted him to come back 'fired up' so that they in turn could get fired up. And so he always did it this way, he would get the sermons prepared first and out of the way. Then he could sit by the pool and relax for the rest of his stay.

It was not until the early hours of Sunday morning that he closed the books. Hungry now, he sought out the fridge and made himself a sandwich. Then he moved into to the lounge where he switched on the TV to search for some late night viewing. He wasn't hopeful.

My dad was right; there never is anything good on TV after ten, he thought as the screen lit up.

He watched two programmes that were really junk viewing, switching from a reality show called 'What happens in Vegas?' to another show called 'Family from Hell'. He liked watching reality shows. They gave him material that he could use in his sermons because they mostly depicted people who were living sinful lives. Sometimes, however, the stories he told in church were not real but were just made up. He'd take one of these people whose lifestyle was exposed in a reality show and then use their story and personality but add a happy ending. One week, he told a story about a boy called Johnny who, he said, had committed the worst kind of sins. This boy then, one night in a dream, had a visit from an angel and so he began coming to church, and this resulted in his abusive parents also making similar changes in their lives. It was all a lie of course, all except the part about Johnny as he had seen him on the TV. But, whether true or not, his stories always seemed to give people in the church hope and encouragement,

That's my job, he thought to himself, *I'm their shepherd.*

After a few hours work, he felt his eyes start to close so he decided to head to bed. He went upstairs and headed towards the west wing. He would not be sharing a room with his wife. Besides, she would have already put all his stuff in the west wing and unpacked everything for him. For both of them, getting a holiday away always meant a holiday away from each other too. Although they were polite to each other and got things done, they were in many ways strangers to each other. They just worked together for the 'greater good'. That lifestyle suited him fine.

Just as he expected, his pyjamas were laid out on the bed awaiting him. His toothbrush and shaver were all set out ready for him. It was what normally happened; it was what his wife did. There would be no need to thank her. It was just the way it was, no more, no less.

His plan for the next few days was to get the sermons done and get started into the relaxation as soon as possible. As he prepared himself for bed, he began to think of Sandra again and remembered that he had not responded to her emails yet, so he took a mental note to do that first thing in the morning.

Silas, often referred to as 'The Butcher', had already served five years of his sentence without getting parole. Nobody ever crossed him in the prison yard. He had made his name through the way he handled those who came against him. Whether in prison or not, his retaliation had always been bitter, brutal and destructive. If five people attacked him, he would then take those five people one by one and do all he could to utterly destroy them. In the past he had beaten up some, and even killed others. His greatest inspiration came from Hollywood revenge movies. Yesterday during the usual Saturday outing to the prison yard, something unexpected had happened. A riot had broken out between two of the main gangs in the prison and several prisoners and officers had got injured in the melee.

Silas himself was out in the yard at the time and was keeping to himself when a member of one of the gangs came up behind him and stabbed him in the back. Silas was no wimp. He was a strong well-built man with the upper body strength of a professional weight-lifter. By a stroke of luck, the prison-made knife, made from an old toothbrush, hit bone and didn't penetrate any further. His assailant wasn't so lucky. Before he could strike again, Silas turned in an instant, grabbed the man in a stranglehold and snapped his neck clean in two.

Later it turned out that his assailant had been no subordinate gang member but one of the 'family' and a central figure of the gang. It was an international gang which extended its influence well beyond the prison walls to the whole nation and even as far as the drug fields of Columbia. Silas soon discovered that he had inadvertently put a price on his own head. Although he knew he could hold his own in a fight, he admitted to himself that they could sneak up on him at any time or even pay off some prison guard to do it. He knew that he was in trouble, to say the least.

Thankfully, the prison guards had experienced enough trouble and had decided to take action. They put most of the senior gang members into solitary confinement, but Silas had spent the night in the infirmary at the prison with his stab wound bandaged up. In the morning they decided to move Silas, first to get further medical attention for his wound and then to transfer him to a new high-security prison that had just been opened, a prison specifically designed for violent prisoners like him. Once there, he would occupy a cell all by himself and not be allowed to mingle with other prisoners for the duration of his sentence which, up to then, seemed to be always increasing due to his infractions. This treatment was designed to force him and other aggressive prisoners to take stock of their lives. Experiments with the method in various prisons over the previous ten years had proved to be quite successful.

So now, Silas found himself sitting in the back of a transport bus, securely strapped in and accompanied by not two but six prison guards. He was seated at the very back of the bus in an internal security cage to separate him from the prison guards just in case he might try anything while they were on the move. The windows of the bus also had a thick wire mesh covering them so that even if someone did break the glass it would be impossible to climb out through the window.

I guess they want to make sure I get to where I'm being sent, he thought.

When he had heard about the transfer, he was glad in the sense that he knew that he would be safer there. On the other hand, he was not quite sure about being locked up by himself. Maybe it would drive him mad, especially if there was no TV to watch revenge movies on.

This is going to be tough, he had admitted as the bus moved off.

The bus headed directly for the nearest place where medical treatment could be found, the hospital in the town of Hope. It was just an hour's drive away.

Soon they were already half way there and had begun to descend the hill leading down into the valley where Hope was located. The authorities had taken every precaution. Only the best guards had been sent, those who were well-trained in physical combat. In fact there was a mixture of experienced veterans and some young-bloods who were reckoned to have sufficient strength to overpower Silas should he try anything when they got to the hospital and had to leave the bus. However, none of this would save them.

Turning a corner at speed, one of the front tyres of the bus suddenly blew out. The bus swerved off the road, tumbled down a steep bank and plunged into the river below. When it hit the water, the front of the bus immediately went straight under the water and got snagged on the river bottom and so the bus was left standing straight up in the water. All of the guards drowned as water flooded in through the broken windows. Their exit was blocked by the bars covering the windows and also by the internal cage. The driver had been knocked-out clean by the impact and he was the only one with the keys. Silas however, was now left hanging precariously by the straps on his seat but held safely in place above the water level. The bus was standing upright so he was safe for now but it began to creak as loud noises came from somewhere under water.

Any second now, this could all give way and I'll be a goner just like the rest of them, he thought.

In truth he knew that his life had been spared within inches of certain death.

All those guards lived good lives. They're gone and me with my life, I'm still alive. Even if I do live through this, my karma will come and get me. Then I'll be gone too.

He said this over and over to himself.

He managed to reach for the buckle of his seatbelt and released himself. He fell down onto the cage. From there he climbed up along the seats to the one directly inside the rear doors. Then he lay on his back against the seat, kicked out and smashed the windows. Glass fell down towards his face but he shielded himself with his arm. He brushed the glass off and began to call out for help through the metal grid. By then he had realised that whatever had caught the front of the bus must be really holding it in place.

Hours went by with him calling out through the broken windows but nobody answered. He began to feel hungry. Prison meals were always on time and his stomach was not used to having to wait. This only agitated him all the more. He could hear the birds chirping in the trees at the top of the bank, also the soft swishing of the river and the odd car driving by above him on the road.

Amazingly, the freak accident hadn't left a single mark on the road except a small tyre mark close to the verge. There had been no barrier to stop them and so, little could be seen from above to show there was anything out of place.

Towards morning, Silas fell into a deep sleep, his breathing barely audible above the sound of a river below his feet. Having shouted until his throat was hoarse, he had finally slept out of sheer exhaustion.

However, when Silas opened his eyes, he found himself lying flat on the green grass of a small hill. He rolled over. It was a beautiful sunny day. All around him there was evidence of life and he watched as small insects moved up and down the grass between his fingers. A large dragonfly flew about his head for a few seconds and then disappeared. He saw everything was in such graphic detail, or perhaps he was just starting to see the details of the world that all along he had been taking for granted.

He stood up and looked around. There was no sign of a river.

How did I get here? he wondered.

He heard the sound of laughter, the laughter of a girl. He began to walk towards the sound. Beyond some hedges he found a playground. It was deserted except for one little girl who was happily swinging on a chain-and-wood swing while giggling away to herself.

"Eh hello," he said hoarsely, noticing how his own voice sounded harsh from all the yelling that he had done.

She stopped laughing, turned her head and just stared at him.

He felt as if her eyes were piercing him like a hot iron.

"Is your mum around, little girl?" he asked.

She shook her head.

"And she lets you out all by yourself?"

She shook her head again.

Silas didn't know what to do. For some reason he felt protective of this little girl although he did not understand why. Nor had he ever seen her before.

"I have a secret," she declared as she began to swing again.

Silas edged forward and asked, "What is it?"

"Push me and I might tell you," she instructed.

Silas began to push her but, as he did, strange thoughts started to rush through his mind about all the bad things that he had ever done. He stopped pushing the swing and turned his head away.

"What's wrong?" she enquired.

"It's nothing" lied Silas, not wanting to discuss murders he had committed with this little innocent girl.

"Fine! I won't tell you the secret then," she said and began to swing away with her face turned away from him.

"Okay, okay," he said having let curiosity get to him, but it was more than ordinary curiosity, more like an instinctive need to know the secret that she spoke about.

"I've been a bad man. I've done bad things," he said humbly.

"Oh," she said, "that's okay. It will all be okay. You'll see."

"All will be ok, will it? People are probably looking for me right now. They may even shoot me dead!"

She stared at him blankly, and he realised that he wasn't going to get a response to what he had just said.

"So tell me then, what is the secret?"

She motioned for him to come closer and, when he leaned forward she whispered in his ear, "The key is in your pocket."

"What?" he frowned.

"The KEY is in your pocket," she repeated, more distinctly this time.

"But..."

Then the green fields began to dim. The entire world went dark and...

Silas woke from his dream and looked around him to find that he was still stuck in the bus. Dawn was about to break and he still hadn't found a way out of the bus.

That dream was so real, he thought, *I wish I was free right now.*

"The key is in my pocket, as if..."

Reaching down, he could feel something in his pocket, something small. He pulled it out to see what it was. Sure enough, it was a key.

"What the?" gasped Silas.

Reaching up from where he was, Silas put the key into the back door. It opened with ease.

He climbed out through the door and stood on the back of the bus. Then he jumped off into the river and, just as he did, the bus dislodged itself, fell flat and began to drift away with the current, sinking as it went.

CHAPTER 3

A GROWING HOPE

Sarah had slept very little since Thursday, and now, once again she lay awake in bed. All through the weekend she had been thinking over what John had said. She had glued herself to the TV several times over the weekend but there had been no report saying that Luke Tyrell had survived the crash. They did not know where the plane had gone down let alone begun a search for survivors. Now with Monday's shift ahead of her, she had started to think that she would have to ask John about it. She was well aware that, if she got caught, she might be accused of promoting the 'delusions' of those she was supposed to be helping. She could argue that it wasn't delusion but reality, but that's not a route that one should ever take when dealing with people who have worked in the field of psychology.

They'd probably end up assessing me, God forbid, she thought to herself.

She arrived at work at eleven and reported to the head nurse who then assigned her to the east wing. There were two psychiatric wards in the hospital, the east wing and the south ward. John was in the south ward.

Damn, she thought to herself as she lifted up her list of patients and went about getting stuck into her work.

It was a long day. Four new patients had come in and they needed full assessments. As well as them, all the other patients had to get their medications and their baths. At two in the afternoon, one of her new patients actually attempted to escape out of the ward. He ran out through the doors and down the corridor into the other parts of the hospital with his clothing rising into the air as he ran, alarming several other patients in various parts of the building. The head nurse came down and reprimanded her and the other staff, and as soon as they got him back the patient was sedated and strapped to a bed in one of the private rooms. After the incident was over, Sarah decided to take a short break and so she left the ward and went outside to sit in the garden for a while.

The hospital garden was quite majestic. It had been designed over a hundred years previously and covered several acres of ground. In modern times, the grounds nearest the hospital were carefully maintained whilst the rest was left to grow wild. In the maintained areas there were flower beds and benches and even a smoking area for those few people who still smoked. The garden gave a kind of holistic feel to the hospital and nurses would sometimes take certain patients out there to give them a break from hospital life. This was especially true in the case of patients in the psychiatric wards as some of these would certainly go 'loopy' after staring at the same four walls for too long. There was also a small children's play area with swings. Sarah went and sat there still trying to calm her nerves as she watched a father pushing his daughter on a swing and gave them a smile.

"Come on," said the father to the child, "let's go and see how your mum is doing."

Then as she watched them walk back towards the hospital entrance, she noticed John on his way out. He was in a wheel chair and was being pushed by Margie Henshaw who was one of the staff nurses. Margie pushed John all the way over to her and then stopped short. Sarah looked questioningly at her.

"He said he wouldn't shut up unless I brought him out here to you," she said, sounding irritated.

Sarah frowned.

"How did he know I was here?"

"No idea."

"Oh."

"Will you...?"

"Oh yes, I'll walk him around for a while and then bring him back in."

"Great," muttered Margie and quickly headed back into the hospital.

"Hi John," said Sarah with a smile.

He smiled back, his eyes gleaming.

"Come on then," she said and began to push him along the path.

She noticed then that his arms had been strapped to the wheelchair.

Margie must have been thinking that he might make a run for it, she thought to herself.

"So, how are you today John?" she asked gently.

"Alright," he replied.

They continued on down along the path until they reached a grassy area with a big oak tree in the middle of it. John motioned with his hand to stop and she did.

"What is it?" she asked.

John just mumbled something under his breath.

"Listen John, I have a question for you..." she said as she stooped to get down to his eye-level.

"I heard what you said last week about the plane and about Luke. I don't know if you have heard the news since, but a plane has gone missing with a famous musician on board called Luke. Is this what you were talking about?"

He nodded.

"But I don't understand. How was it possible for you to know what was going to happen?"

"Ever since I was a child," he said slowly, "my father has been telling me many things, things just like that."

"Your father?"

He nodded again.

Strange, she thought, standing up to push him some more.

His answer had made her more mystified than ever.

Suddenly John turned his head and said, "You know Sarah, you have to help me."

"What do you mean?"

"You are the one! You are to take me out into the garden and set me free."

She stopped walking and stood in front of him.

"No!" she exclaimed, making a point to make eye contact with him, "I can't do that, John, I'd lose my job!"

John said nothing for a while but just sat there looking down at his arm straps.

"Just take me back inside then," he said defiantly.

She turned the wheel chair around and pushed him back to the ward. Nothing more was said between them that day.

Harold awoke with a start. His alarm clock was bleeping, indicating that it was time for him to get up for work. He sat up and put his feet on the cold wooden floor. Their house was an old one and didn't have much insulation nor did it have a great heating system.

Where are my slippers? he thought to himself, looking around for them.

The cold morning was a reminder that summer doesn't last forever and that one should take advantage of it while it is here.

He got up and made his breakfast. No one else in the house was awake yet, so all was quiet. Harold reflected on the dramatic change that had occurred over the past three days ever since he had come home to see Jenny singing for joy. It was as if she had become a new person or that she had come to terms with her new life and the loss of her parents. Maybe she had reverted to behaviour that was normal for her before the trauma. Harold knew that in some ways what was happening was a good thing, but he also had to admit that it was making life more difficult for both him and his wife.

There were other things to consider as well. Tonight his brother Val would be arriving, coming all the way from Connecticut to stay with them for a week. Val hadn't met his new niece yet and Harold was worried about how he would react when he did. As he thought about Val, he remembered that he had been surprised at his call asking them if it was okay to come for a visit, since Harold and Suzie could have counted on the fingers of one hand the number of times they had heard from Val over the previous seven years. Val had been in trouble several years back. Being the younger brother, he had spent more years in care after they had been taken away from their parents. This had left him angry and resentful and he had got mixed up with a bad crowd and, as a result, had done some time in prison. But now, thankfully, he had turned his life around and was travelling around the country for his job although Harold couldn't quite remember what he said he worked at. Val never really talked about it, but whatever it was, it did keep him quite busy.

Harold and Suzie didn't have a spare bedroom so during the weekend, they had prepared a bed in the basement for Val to sleep on. Harold could still feel his arms aching from moving all the junk that had been down there. Normally he didn't spend much time working-out and so the extra effort had left him feeling quite sore.

He went and picked up the mail from the mailbox and sat there opening envelopes while sipping on a second cup of coffee. He liked doing this after breakfast, although the mail didn't always arrive in time for him to do it every morning. He recognised one envelope immediately.

MasterCard bill, he noted to himself.

He opened it and checked down the list of purchases but saw nothing out of order. However, when he opened the next envelope address simply to 'house owner', he found a letter inside from the local school. Scanning through it, he saw that it was an invitation for parents to register a child now with the school for the coming year. The letter mentioned an open day for parents to come along with their children.

Another thing to keep in mind, he thought to himself.

As his mind drifted, he began to imagine what it would be like for Jenny in school, if she went on singing her Jesus songs in a school where such things are banned and defaulters punished.

"She'll be expelled," he said aloud with a laugh, shaking his head.

He left the letter on the table for Suzie to see, put his used dishes in the sink and then left for work.

That evening, on the way home from work, Harold called by the coach station to pick up Val. He was feeling peckish so when he arrived early he went into the supermarket across the street and bought himself a snack to eat while he was waiting. He had called Suzie earlier in the day to check on how things were and during their conversation, Jenny had manoeuvred her way on to the phone to say 'hello' to him, which he thought was very cute. She seemed really excited that Val was coming to stay with them. She kept on saying the word 'uncle' in a way that sounded more like 'ukkel'. As he ate his snack, Harold recalled her words and how she pronounced them and smiled happily to himself. He sat in the car and waited, watching the minutes go by on his watch. The coach turned up thirteen minutes late.

When he saw Val step off the coach he got out of the car to greet him. Though Val was the younger brother he was definitely the taller of the two. In fact, he stood six inches taller.

Age is taking its toll on him, Harold thought as he walked over to him.

Val was beginning to bald. He had also lost weight and walked with a slight limp on his right leg. But his face lit up with a smile when he saw Harold and he happily grabbed him for a man-hug.

"It's been too long, brother," he said, his face beaming.

"It has! It has! But how are you, Val? You're looking..."

"Old! I know," Val interrupted, laughing.

"What happened to your leg?" queried Harold.

"Ah, I did some ligament damage one day on the job."

"Oh, wow! How did that happen?"

"Long story!" said Val in a way that cut off the flow of conversation.

Ignoring the abrupt reply, Harold pointed and said, "The car is this way."

"The town hasn't changed much," Val said as he looked this way and that on the way to the parking lot.

"No not really," agreed Harold. Then turning to Val, he asked him, "How many years has it been since you were here?"

"It's about a year I think, I came down for a weekend, remember? But you guys were away and I didn't get to see you."

"Oh yeah, that's right. We had gone down to Florida for a couple of weeks."

They reached the parking bay where Harold had left his car. He unlocked it and put Val's bags into the trunk.

"So how is she? My niece?" Val asked as they sat into the car.

"Good, yeah, things were tough at first but they seem to be getting better now."

"That's good!"

As soon as they were on the road Val drifted off into his thoughts and casually watched the town go by. He wasn't quite sure about how he was going to talk to Harold about Jenny but he was looking forward to seeing her again. He knew that there was a risk that he was under surveillance so he had taken the precaution not to come and visit her until four or five weeks after she had been placed with Harold and Suzie. Harold knew nothing about his part in setting up the placement, nor did he know that Val and Jenny were no strangers to each other. This was all part of a bigger plan that they were all going to have to fit into.

The car pulled into the drive and Harold beeped the horn. Immediately Suzie and Jenny came running out to greet them. Jenny ran straight to her uncle and he lifted her up and gave her a big hug.

"It's good to see you again," he whispered in her ear and then lowered her to the ground.

She smiled happily and took him by the hand.

"Come on, uncle," she said gleefully as she pulled him in the direction of the house.

Val shrugged his shoulders and walked with her.

"She must be good with strangers," he said offhandedly to Suzie in case his action aroused suspicion that he and Jenny were more acquainted than she and Harold realised.

Jenny led him right into the lounge and began showing him some of the things that her new parents had bought for her. Harold and Suzie followed and Val took the opportunity to greet Suzie properly with a hug and a little kiss on her cheek. Soon Jenny ran off to fetch more toys from her room.

"Well now," Val said to Harold and Suzie, "aren't you two blessed with such a wonderful little girl?"

Suzie nodded. She was glad to hear him say this.

Jenny ran back into the room. Harold quickly noticed how preoccupied Jenny was with her uncle and he began to think that perhaps Val would be able to distract her and keep her from her constant songs and prayers. Suddenly, however, Jenny stopped playing and started to pray out loud. When she finished, Val said 'amen' with her.

Harold and Suzie stood there, too stunned to say a word. Then Val broke the silence.

"Guys, you should really say 'amen' when Jenny prays. You know, give her that bit of encouragement."

In truth, Harold was totally and utterly shocked. Having thought that Val might go and report them when he found out what Jenny was doing, here he was instead, asking them to encourage Jenny. He realised that it had been a total miscalculation on his part.

I guess Val always was anti-establishment, he thought to himself.

Later, when Harold and Suzie left the room to prepare for dinner, Val stayed, sitting quietly. He was pondering when might be the best time to tell them the real truth about Jenny.

Mr Balding arrived at the airport. He climbed out of the taxi, handed the driver thirty dollars for the fare and asked for a receipt.

The first of my expenses, he thought as he carefully put it away in his wallet.

He had spent the weekend researching the so called 'fanatics' before ringing the commissioner back to take the job. He had thoroughly read through all the files at least twice, and referred back to various parts a third time while doing his own searches online. The files concerned people who were suspected to be involved in this radical religious group who were meeting secretly. The files had many details; it seemed as if the investigation had been tracking them through their online activity. Their emails and social networks were being tracked, something which also provided photos for many of them. However, the investigation thus far had failed to match any of them to official documents such as marriage certificates, birth certificates, hospital records, passports or driving licences. The investigators had searched using every conceivable method. They had used the latest technology but had drawn a blank. Yet, amazingly, here were those 'fanatics' openly using unofficial websites, with their full names and even photos. The only conclusion that Mr Balding could make was that they couldn't be using their real names. So, as he thought this over, he realised that if he was ever going to locate them he would have to try and discover their true identities. He studied their photos to try and work out their ages, and then their profiles to try to learn all he could about them. More subtly by creating a fake account, he even befriended some of them on those social networks. By this method, he would get daily updates on their profiles, information which might give him clues as he progressed with his investigation.

Following the sign saying 'Departures', Mr Balding went in through the entrance of the airport and headed over towards the check-in area. He had chosen to fly with Key West Airlines, a small company but he didn't mind as it was only going to be a short flight down to Hope Municipal Airport. Hope only had a small airstrip and so none of the bigger planes used by the larger commercial airlines were able to land there. He stood at the desk and waited for service but no-one was there. He dropped his bags on the floor and started to look around. It had been a while since he had flown anywhere. The airport had only changed a little; it still had the same layout but some of the shops had changed.

"Hello sir."

He turned back to see that a girl was now seated behind the desk so he stepped up and handed her his documents. She took them from him and started typing the details into her computer.

"I'm sorry, sir," she said apologetically, "I don't think your flight will be leaving today."

"What?" said Balding, his anger already rising at the possibility of a delay.

She pointed up at the display on the screens behind him in the departure lounge. Most of them read either 'Delayed' or 'Cancelled'. With drops of sweat appearing on his forehead, he turned back to face the girl.

"What's going on?" he demanded, "what's happened with all the flights?"

"Didn't you hear about the flight that was lost and is thought to have ditched in the sea?"

"Yes I think I saw it on the news," he answered, still not sure how this could have any connection to his travel plans.

She continued, "There are suspicions that it might have been caused by a terrorist attack. Since yesterday they have been restricting both inbound and outbound flights at all airports in this part of the country."

"You're kidding!" he said.

"No sir."

"What about my flight? It's only a small plane, right? Can't we just go?"

She shook her head.

"This is not good enough," he retorted. "I want to speak with your superior."

"It won't do any good talking to him," she replied, "it's the airport authority people that you'd need to speak to."

Mr Balding snatched his tickets back out of her hands, grabbed his suitcases and walked back fifteen feet away from her desk. He pulled out the stealth phone from his pocket and rang the police commissioner's number.

"Balding..."

"Commissioner ..."

"Everything okay?"

"I'm at the airport and I'm having difficulty getting a flight. It seems that the whole place has been shut down."

"Yeah," said the commissioner, "its crazy here too as we have had the added pressure of putting extra police in position out there at the airport. Nothing I can do for you on this one I'm afraid. Where were you headed anyway?"

"To Hope," answered Balding, "it's a small town a few hundred miles away."

"Then, why don't you drive there?" asked the commissioner.

"I guess I could but I'd have to rent a car. My own car wouldn't be up to that kind of journey. But, remember, I'm putting it all on your tab."

"Whatever you need," said the commissioner without hesitation.

"Good then, we'll talk again later," Balding replied still trying to adjust his mind to the unexpected change of plans.

"Bye!" said the commissioner and the line went dead.

Mr Balding strolled over to the car-hire desk and leaned in over the desk looking for immediate attention.

"I need a car," he blurted out as soon as the receptionist looked up at him.

Linda stirred the stew she was making. It had been brewing for some time now and was almost ready. Her mum had taught her this recipe and it was very nutritious. She normally only cooked it during the winter but, after the way that the children had been lately and with her own low energy levels, she wanted to help everyone get back into a good state of health as soon as possible.

She lifted down the plates and got out the cutlery.

"George. Come and set the table please," she called.

He didn't come straightaway and, as she was in a get-things-done-now kind of mood, she went ahead and set the table herself - just a simple layout, with knives and forks, and sauces for the children. The children had a particular fondness for tomato ketchup but she had never really liked it, even in her own childhood. Sam, of course, ate 'buckets' of the stuff.

Must be where the children get it from, she thought as she checked that everything was in place for the meal.

"Dinner's ready," she called, loud enough to be heard in the next room.

She gathered the plates and was just about to start serving when she realised she couldn't hear the children coming. Normally they would have come running at the mention of food.

She went into the lounge which was adjacent to the kitchen with no door between the two. To her surprise, the children weren't there. Even her youngest had apparently been removed from his walker and was gone as well.

"Dinner's ready," she called again as she began ascend the staircase.

She walked into the children's bedroom and found them standing together in a circle. Damon, the smallest, was being held in place by George and Jason and they were holding each other by the hand.

"What on earth are you doing?" demanded Linda angrily.

They dropped their hands at the sound of her voice and looked at her.

"Nothing, just playing," said George in answer to her question.

"Didn't you hear me?" she asked, "I called you ages ago. Dinner is ready!"

"Sorry mum!" said George and Jason together as they made a dash to the kitchen.

That's more like it, she thought.

She went and picked up Damon off the floor and carried him down to the kitchen and put him in his high-chair. Then, she served the stew and placed the plates one by one in front of the boys.

"Might be a bit hot," she cautioned.

After serving herself, she sat down at the table and was just about to start eating when George stopped her and asked, "May I say grace, mum?"

"Err, sure honey," she said puzzled at this new development.

She watched as George bowed his head and prayed with a clear voice, "Dear God, please bless this food. And bless this house and my family. And bless the hands that made such nice food. In Jesus' name, amen."

The other two, who had both waited, now tucked into their food in their usual manner.

As Linda ate her dinner, she kept thinking about what George had done and also the words he had used.

They never wait for grace!

Grace was something that their dad would have taught them to say at mealtimes but he was never able to stop them from grabbing a mouthful or two first.

They must be missing their dad, she thought, still trying to find an explanation for the sudden change in their behaviour. It didn't help that she had been unsuccessful in all attempts to reach him since their argument the other day.

"We could try to get your dad on Skype tonight," she offered, partly to see what their reaction might be.

George just smiled, nodded and continued to eat his food.

To give herself time to think, Linda ate her food slowly. It tasted just as it should and felt good going down. Taking out her phone from her pocket, she sent a text to Sam telling him that the children wanted to talk to him on Skype that evening.

She lifted her eyes and looked across the table at the boys and thought about how lucky she was to have children like them. In truth, she loved each of them dearly. When she and Sam had first discussed the idea of having children, she had originally been somewhat reluctant, but now she was very happy with the decision that they had made.

"Mum, the ketchup is all gone," complained George.

"Oh, let me go and see," she said, getting up. She checked the cupboard and discovered they hadn't any more.

"I'm sorry," she said as she came back to the table, "we'll have to get more from the store."

George put down his spoon and folded his arms in frustration.

"Would you like to try some barbeque sauce?"

"No."

There was nothing more she could do so she made her apology and then sat down to finish her own dinner.

As she did, she watched George lift up the bottle of ketchup and hold it under the table. She kept on eating, leaving him free to try and squeeze some more sauce out of the bottle. Within seconds, amazingly, she heard the sound of sauce being squeezed on to a plate. She looked over and was astounded to see George happily covering his food with ketchup. What had been an empty container was now half full.

"Let me see that," Linda demanded, reaching over and snatching it from his hands.

She examined it. The bottle was definitely half full.

Was it only blocked? she thought, doubting whether she had seen an empty bottle only a few moments earlier.

Stunned, she sat there in silence, holding the sauce bottle in her hand as George got busy eating.

Mr Smith sat down on his sofa and opened up the evening paper. It was coming to the end of his first day off work and he was settling into a relaxed routine. He had taken his time in making his travel arrangements but just the previous evening he had checked out the travel details and discovered that even though there was flights normally operating between Washington and Hope, there was flight restrictions to the South East where he wanted to get to and so he would have to drive if he really wanted to get there. He had debated the issue in his mind all evening before he had slept, and the same debate was continuing now as he put his feet up on the coffee table. He knew that it would be a serious undertaking if he were to drive to Hope as it was in the region of twelve hundred miles away. He really wasn't altogether fond of long journeys by car. This was due to something that was deep in his psyche, rooted in his boyhood resentment of his dad taking him on long drives in the countryside when all he wanted to do was stay home and play his video games.

He scanned the front page of the paper. The headline read 'Terror Attacks Imminent!'. He noticed that the paper had a special pullout section giving details of the flight that was still missing. He pulled it out and read through the article. It outlined where the searches were being conducted and even gave names of some of the people who had been on board. It seemed that there were several people of note on the plane but the newspaper was focusing on one particular man named James, an infamous blogger. Apparently, this man had a huge online following because he had once exposed a scandal amongst some of the most popular politicians of the time. Thinking back, Mr Smith could remember the incident happening two years previously and he had seen its impact in Washington first-hand. Somehow James had managed to secure minutes of secret meetings that were being held without the knowledge of the majority of public representatives. In these minutes, there were references to money-laundering and other illegal activities. After the scandal blew over, many people had thought that James would have run for a seat in the following election, but, instead he left the country and travelled around the world. Apparently this flight had been the last part of his journey home and the plane had mysteriously disappeared. The paper was hinting left, right and centre at possible conspiracies. Mr Smith, knowing how many politicians in Washington felt about this man, knew the potential for this to be a real conspiracy. It was similar to how people in jail hate those who tell on them and call them 'rats'. It doesn't matter that what they were doing was wrong.

It only matters that the person told on them and he is hated for doing so.

His phone rang so he put the paper down and looked at the screen. The caller I.D. read, 'Lisa'.

He refused to let himself answer it, and pressed the 'ignore' key.

Moments later a text came through from her. It read 'Where are you? I need you!'

Her message was enough to push him to make his decision and leave. He finished his cup of coffee in one gulp and got moving, packing enough clothes for a month even though he actually didn't know how long he would be gone. He could stay away for an indefinite time if he so chose. Just before leaving the house, he went over to his bed, reached underneath it and started to pull out some boxes. He eventually found a dusty old blue shoe box and laid it carefully on to the bed and opened it. Inside there were a pack of old photos and a set of keys. He took the keys and put them into his pocket and then closed the shoebox and put it and all the other boxes, back neatly under his bed. He lifted his suitcase and was just about to open the door when suddenly an impulse came over him - more like a prompt - to leave his phone behind. He pulled it out of his pocket, placed it on the counter and left.

Silas scrambled into the woods. His cold wet clothes were clinging to his body. He was very aware that his orange prison outfit would be quite visible if they came looking for him and he knew it would only be a matter of time before they did. While finding his way through the forest, the terrain was uneven and Silas found himself walking up quite steep hills. The bushes got denser the further he went. Going through one dense patch of bushes, thorns tore his right arm and he immediately felt the stinging pain of ripped skin. Nevertheless, the freedom, the fresh air and the open countryside felt good to this man who had been locked up for years. Yet, here he was, free! He was hopeful that the authorities might think that he had been drowned in the bus and that his body had floated away down the river. He hoped that everyone might think that he was dead.

I'll need to keep low, and off the radar if I can, he thought to himself.

He kept moving forwards at a steady pace not wanting to push himself too hard nor, at the same time, to get too close to any other person. It would be far from ideal if he were to bump into anyone in the woods because that would mean that his presence would be discovered. He could kill the person but then there would be a missing person and that would put the police on alert. It wouldn't take them long to connect the two things, a missing person and an escaped convict.

Suddenly there was a loud crack as his footing gave way underneath him and he slid down a small slope and into a pile of dead undergrowth. He got up and brushed himself off, thankful not to have sprained his ankle or worse.

He knew that there was a town down below him in the valley, and a town meant a place where he could find clothes and food. He also knew that it would more than likely have cops and, if indeed they were looking for him, then this town could well be the place where the search teams would set up a base. He decided to change direction and climb to higher ground in order to get a better view of the valley below. At the top of a large hill he climbed a tree and from there he was able to see everything clearly. Sure enough, there was the town, positioned by the side of a large lake. A river meandered down the valley and flowed through the centre of the town and into the lake. The forest continued right up to and around the town except on the east side where there seemed to be some farms and a small airstrip. To the west of the lake there were a few cabins, built along the edge of the lake. Silas smiled. This was what he wanted to find.

I might find an empty lodge over there and have shelter and maybe even locate some clothes and food, he thought to himself.

He tried to estimate the distance from where he was and reckoned that the cabins were still at least about ten miles away. Having got his bearings, he climbed down. He knew how to get to the cabins he had seen. He would keep along to the west of the lake and, when he got there, he would see if he could get supplies out of any of the cabins that were unoccupied. He walked on, edging his way slowly downwards and to the west but after a few miles, his legs began to tire. He found another stream and stopped there for a drink. The forest he had passed through had been completely devoid of any source of sustenance. In other forests he might have found camping items left behind or discarded food but not here. This was a place free of tourists and the wildlife was left alone. Actually, it had once been a place where people came to hunt wild animals but that was before the area was designated as a nature reserve.

The water in the stream was cold yet tasted fresher than any bottled water. Refreshed, Silas stood up again. He didn't want to go into the water as his orange suit had almost dried but he knew that he had to. He forced himself to go in and walk downstream for about fifty yards.

This will help cover my tracks if they have dogs tracking me, he thought.

He took special care not to slip on the rocks under his feet. However, by the time he climbed back on to the bank, he could hardly feel his ankles because they were so cold.

It was beginning to get dark so he walked on as he had no way of keeping warm if he stopped. Soon, the sun went down and a full moon crept up into the sky and its light gave him assistance to keep making his way through the forest. Shadows from the trees made weird shapes and several times he stopped thinking that he had seen someone only to realise that it was just the shadows playing tricks on him. The night had brought with it a sharp drop in temperature and he was certainly feeling it. His prison-issue trainers were still wet and every soggy step made his feet ache. He stumbled on through the night, no longer sure of his direction anymore. Then, suddenly, out of the blue, he came across a cabin.

No lights from the windows, he noticed.

He circled the cabin, remaining under the cover of the trees. There was no car and no sign of life. He approached the building cautiously. As he stepped on to the porch, it creaked beneath his feet. He stopped and listened but there was only silence. All he could hear was the sighing of the wind in the trees. He moved forward and slowly turned the handle of the door. It opened.

Inside he was greeted by a musty smell and by a collection of large cobwebs. He knocked over a few empty cans on the floor and this made a loud racket. There was still no reaction from anybody.

Great! The place is deserted.

He left the door open, using the light of the moon to help his search of the cabin. He found matches and an oil lamp and lit it. Then, after shutting the door, he had a proper look around. On first inspection there was not much there except layers of dust but under the bed he found an old jacket. He dusted it down, shook off some insects and then placed it around his shoulders. It felt good. He smirked at the idea of a dirty motheaten jacket feeling good. He sat down on the edge of the one and only bed. One leg of it was broken and the mattress felt like a rock.

What a day! he thought, as he cupped his hands around the lamp.

After he had warmed up a little, he continued his search of the cabin and found more useful things. There was an old penknife in the sink, more matches by the fireplace, and a water canteen hanging behind the door. He knew the value of these items for his survival. He removed his wet shoes and put them near the lamp and then he crawled into the bed, pulling an old blanket he had found over himself.

On a beach, a father and daughter were out for an evening stroll. As he father walked, the little girl ran back and forth allowing herself to be chased by the waves as they hit the beach. Often when they went walking on the beach, they would see all kinds of things washed up. This day was no different and the father had spotted something ahead, something quite big which was still being touched by the very edge of the waves. A first he thought that it could be a small whale or some kind of fish, but as they drew close, he could make out the figure of a human being. He immediately stopped walking and called his daughter over to him. Then he told her to face the other direction because he feared that it might be a dead body that they had discovered and didn't want her to see it. Leaving her there, he walked over to the body. As he knelt down to have a look, he noticed that the man was still breathing. He quickly grabbed the man under the arms and dragged him away from the reach of the water. Other people who were out walking or jogging on the beach, saw the commotion and came over to see what was going on. The father let the man rest on his side and he began to shake him to see if he would wake.

"Senor?" he called.

"Senor!" he repeated, shaking the man again and again. Eventually, the man rolled on to his back and opened his eyes. He looked around, bewildered, unsure where he was. A small crowd was now gathered around him.

They watched as the man rolled back on to his side, coughed and spat water out of his mouth.

One person took their towel and covered the man's body to help warm him up a little.

"Where am I?" the man asked with a hoarse voice.

"Como?" said the dad, not understanding English.

"Mehico?" the man prompted, trying to make Mexico sound Spanish.

The dad nodded, smiling. At last they were communicating.

The man pointed at his own chest and introduced himself, "My name - Luke" he said.

Then he reached up so that the dad could help him to his feet.

CHAPTER 4

MYSTERY OF HOPE

Silas awoke. The room was bright due to the sunlight that was streaming in through the windows so he got up. First, he checked through each window to make sure that no one was around and then he took the canteen and walked back as far as the stream to get some water. The main thing on his mind, now that he had found somewhere to stay for the time being, was food. He weighed up the possibility of going on further to try and find some more dwellings. Maybe he could find a cabin or two left unlocked and take some food out of them. This idea, of course, faced him with the risk of being discovered, reported and then captured by the police. Nevertheless, his belly was aching; it was calling out for food. He had to go.

Back at the cabin, he found some old coffee that was so old that it was almost stuck to the tin but he managed to scrape some out with a spoon and, with the log burner lit, he soon made himself a hot drink. He found little else of much use except a very looking old tin of canned food without a label on it. He used his knife to open it and found it contained peaches. He wondered for a moment if they were still safe to eat but, by now, he was so hungry that he decided to eat them whether they were fresh or not. He quickly ate half way through them then he made himself stop in order to save some for later because he had no idea where or when he would find more food to eat.

As soon as he felt his energy return enough for him to venture out properly, he threw a few logs on the fire, grabbed his belongings and started to walk in a westerly direction again. He tried to make a mental note of the various landmarks and turns so that he could easily find his way back later. After walking for an hour, he began to realise how remote the cabin he'd stayed in was. It was probably only reachable on foot or by four-by-four vehicles.

He jumped down into a small stream and steadied himself against an overhanging tree. He was just about to climb up the opposite bank when in the corner of his eye he caught the glimpse of a face. It was there, and then it was gone. It was a face that he had seen before but couldn't remember where.

He walked on, thinking perhaps his mind must have been playing tricks on him but, after a while, he began to remember the face. It was one of his victims from several years before, an elderly woman who lived a house that he had broken into. He had robbed her of all her money, tied her up and then left her there. Three days later on the news he saw that she had been found barely alive. He could even recall the sneering remark that he had made about her. His stomach rumbled again and he began to wonder what it would have been like to go without food for three whole days. He took out the peaches and ate the rest of them. However, he kept visualising the woman tied up for three days without food and wondered what if it had been the other way around and he was the one left to starve.

My belly hurts so badly right now, he thought, *it must have been real tough on that old lady.*

The more he thought about her, the more he began to feel remorse and regret for what he had done.

"I'm sorry old lady for doing that to you," he said out loud as if he were apologising to her face to face.

As he said the words, a strange feeling of warmth came over him and he could feel tears form in his eyes.

Suddenly realising what he'd just said, he shook off and idea of making an apology.

"What's wrong with you, Silas?" he said to himself, "come on, I need food and I need it soon."

He began walking again. About two hundred feet further on, he came across the boundary of a property. It was another cabin. This one however was accessed by a lane and there was a car parked in the drive outside. Silas crouched and studied the scene from behind the bushes. He noticed that there seemed to be elderly couple occupying the cabin so he waited and, soon enough, the lady drove off in the car. Silas moved towards the cabin from a side which wasn't overlooked by windows and then worked his way around to the back door. The handle turned with ease and he opened the door and went straight into the kitchen. Quickly he began to take items from the fridge, some of this and some of that but nothing too substantial so as to draw attention to having been there. Just then he accidentally dislodged a packet of ham and it made a small noise as it hit the floor.

"Is that you dear?" he heard a man call.

He quickly picked up the ham and put it back into the fridge, then paused to consider what to do.

What if I knocked this old man out? he wondered. *I need food badly and besides, he might see me leaving.* Just then, Silas heard a car pull up and he instinctively ducked down so as not to be seen. He left quietly by the back door, closing it behind him with care and quickly darted towards the undergrowth. Safely there, he sat and watched for a while but no one came after him and no one even looked out.

That was close, he thought to himself, *way too close!*

Pastor Edgeworth awoke feeling comfortable and refreshed. For a moment he reflected on how greatly he appreciated one of his wife's obsessions, that of putting clean sheets on his bed every day. It had been like that every day of their marriage, and, even on their honeymoon, she had gone to the hotel management to complain about the sheets. But, right now, in this moment of sheer bliss, he was content just to lie there. He had been at the house for three days now and was well and truly settled into holiday mode. Sometimes he would picture his retirement being like this, relaxing in a place of peace away from the hustle and bustle of life. However, he had no inclination to retire until in his sixties. He wanted to make as much money as possible while employed as pastor of his church.

He climbed out of bed and put on his slippers and robe and went downstairs to the kitchen. The breakfast table was all laid out already with everything he would need and with a jug of freshly-squeezed orange juice in the centre.

This is the life, he thought as he sat in to the table.

"Good morning darling," he said to his wife, "what's on the menu?"

"French bread," she announced.

She had already been up for an hour and had everything ready. She came over with some coffee, poured it for him and handed him the morning paper.

"Thanks," he said.

She always got the paper for him.

"A prison escape! Near here!" he gasped.

"Really?" she said.

"Yeah," he said, "it says here Silas also known as 'The Butcher' was being transported to a hospital but the prison-transport bus has gone missing, vanished without a trace and everybody in it. Maybe it's the rapture, like it says in the Bible," he said, laughing at his own joke.

"Where had the bus come from?" asked his wife.

"The state penitentiary, I think," he answered checking back over the article.

"Oh, that must be the one over in the next valley," said his wife trying to remember. She had seen the headline but hadn't read the full story.

"Yeah, I think it must be," said the pastor, "and it's not too far from here."

"Do they think that man could be in this area?" she asked anxiously.

He scanned the article again.

"It says here that it's possible that he had made enemies with some of the local gangs and that they might be responsible for his disappearance. Wow! Six prison guards are missing too. They are calling in state troopers to assist in the search, and the search area will include Hope and also several other local towns. That will take some time, I reckon. We should think about our security here and make sure the doors are locked at night!"

"Yes, we'd better," she agreed nervously.

"Better safe than sorry! I'll talk to the staff today," he said firmly.

By 'staff' he meant the gardener and the lady who did the cleaning. He was never sure why they employed a cleaner when his wife was so particular but perhaps she needed the help.

God only knows, he thought to himself as he checked the other main headlines of the paper. Then his wife brought over his hot food and he put the paper aside. She sat down opposite him and they talked for a while, asking about the day ahead and enquiring what each of them was planning to do.

When she left the kitchen to go get a shower, he picked up the paper again and turned to the gossip column to read some of the letters written by poor unfortunates stuck in their dramatic lives. The stories always brought a smile to his face.

He also had a look at the personal advertisements to see if there were any about local women that might catch his attention. But the local people were quite conservative, not like those in the big city, and so the things were not so blatant. With no ads of interest there, he closed the paper and made a decision to get one of his books from the office and go back to bed to read for a while. He walked down the hall and opened his office door. To his surprise the gardener and cleaner were in there together, not kissing or holding hands. Instead, they were down on their on their hands and knees, crying.

"What the hell do you think you're doing?" demanded the pastor, his voice raised.

They jumped up immediately and turned to face him.

"We were only praying, sir," they explained.

"Praying? In my office? During working hours?"

"We are sorry sir. We just wanted to pray this morning, after hearing the news."

"What news?"

"About the convict who seems to have escaped from the prison bus," said the gardener.

The pastor strode over to stand behind his desk. He turned and glared at the two people in front of him.

"Are you praying for the police to capture him or to shoot him dead before he kills someone else?" he asked with a sneer.

"Eh, no sir," said the cleaner.

"Then what?" said the pastor turning to look at her.

"We were actually praying that he will come to know God."

"Him? A murderer! Come to know God! You must be kidding!"

His anger flared and he barked an order as a master to one of his subordinates, "Come on now the two of you. Get out of here! Play time is over. Go get back to work and don't let me ever find you in here again. If you want to pray, pray on your own time not mine!"

They accepted his rebuke, apologised again and left the room.

The pastor sat down on his chair.

"The nerve of them!" he declared aloud, forgetting all about the book he had planned to read.

Sarah woke up for a second time. It was Tuesday morning so she got up and went to the bathroom and brushed her teeth. About an hour ago she had been stirred her from her sleep by a dream, although she could not quite remember what the dream was about. She stood there staring blankly at her reflection in the mirror and wondered what she would for the day as she did not have to go to work. She still felt a little tired but decided that she did not wish to stay in bed all day and waste it. Tonight, Steve was coming around to see her.

He had been away for the past week – all she knew was that he was some sort of a trucker and this kind of trip was commonplace for him. Finished brushing, she spat toothpaste into the basin, rinsed and then wiped her mouth dry.

Although she didn't want to admit it, the case of John Doe at work still had her mystified. She wondered about his 'condition' and whether it had been properly diagnosed or researched. She remembered how some autistic children, although unable to communicate properly, are then found to be geniuses in other areas such as maths. She had wondered if perhaps John's condition could be something similar. Maybe he had something which made it seem like he was able to see into the future but in reality it was really some form of clever analysis done by solving math's equations or probabilities. It was pure conjecture, but it was her only way of turning the strangeness back into a reality that she could understand. Several times lately, both Sarah and other hospital employees had found John during his 'mad' moments, announcing things only for them to come true or to be already true. The last event was when a new patient had arrived at the hospital and John had shouted out to him, calling him a murderer and saying that he must repent.

How did he know? Only the nurses had known about the murder that the man had committed. There must be a logical explanation, Sarah reflected.

It was possible that he had inadvertently heard the nurses talking about it. Sarah had examined several possible explanations but when the same kind of thing was happening again and again, she had no idea how to explain what was going on. She had talked to the doctor in charge of John's case but he merely recorded John as delusional and prescribed him some pills. However, since taking the pills, John's strange moments had only intensified. Now both the nurses and the other patients tried to avoid him because his behaviour had become more unpredictable than ever.

Sarah wasn't in the mood for breakfast so she got dressed and headed out the door. She had noticed before that there was a library in the town, but despite walking past it several times she had never gone inside. As she walked she started in that direction, planning to do a bit of personal research about John's case. The library was only down at the bottom of her street. It was a fine building with two large pillars out front although, from the outside, it looked as if it needed a paint job. She walked inside and looked around. There was a reception counter and a librarian to her left in front of her stood some reading desks. The books were all stored in rows of shelves over to her right. She walked up to the librarian.

"Hi," she said, "I was wondering if you might be able to help me."

"Yes if I can," answered the librarian, looking up from what she'd been doing.

"I work as a carer at the hospital," she explained. "We have a patient there whose condition is baffling us and I was hoping to do a little research to see if I can find any relevant information."

"Oh I see," said the librarian, "the medical journals and reference books can be found in aisle four. It's over that way," she said, pointing.

Sarah followed the direction and found the section.

After an hour trawling through various books and documents she found nothing that specialised in abnormal psychological conditions. She sighed and went back to the librarian.

"Hi again," she said to get the librarian's attention.

"Any luck?" asked the librarian.

"No, I found nothing. I might need a different kind of book," she sighed.

"I see," said the librarian, "tell me, what kind of condition is it? Can you describe it?"

"I'm not supposed to discuss it. Confidentiality of patients, you know,"

Sarah answered slowly.

"I'm only trying to help," said the librarian.

She doesn't know who I am talking about, so I guess it will be alright, Sarah reflected.

She looked straight at the librarian.

"Okay, but please don't let it go any further. I don't want anyone else is to know."

The librarian nodded.

"I guess you could say that this patient seems to be able to tell the future or at least that he has the mental capacity to make it seem as if he can."

"So he tells you that he can tell the future," said the librarian, trying to verify what Sarah had told her.

"No," Sarah replied, "he just tells the future, or reveals details things about the present. He talks about things when there's no way that he could possibly know about them."

"Hmm," said the librarian thoughtfully.

Sarah could see from her expression that her words had triggered something in the librarian's memory.

"What is it?" she asked.

"Along with being the librarian here, I am also the town's top historian. There is something here that might interest you."

The librarian got up, beckoned and walked away from her desk. Sarah followed her excitedly. The librarian led her over to the history section of the library, searched the shelves and pulled out an old book. It had a brown hard cover and as she opened it, Sarah noticed how the pages had all yellowed with age. The librarian flicked quickly through the book until she found a certain page and then handed the book to Sarah to read.

"The miracles of 1845," Sarah said, reading the title out loud. Then she read on, "In 1845, the outbreak of consumption was particularly bad and there was a large increase in the number of patients coming out of Dallas to the hospital. Among them was a man that caused a great deal of interest. He just called himself John. Doctors and nurses looking after him found that he quickly recovered from the disease and that in itself was nothing less than a miracle. However, following his recovery, he began to visit other patients and, later on, some of them reported that they had been healed. Other patients told stories about how John had known their deepest secrets and also had been able to tell them about their future. One such account was given by a man called Artie Stevens. He was a patient who had also come from Dallas, but he was a relative of a local family living in the town. He claimed that John had told him that he was going to die but that he had been forgiven of all the bad things in his life and not only that but his kin would carry a message of hope for the future. Artie had died the next day. His wife and children stayed in town for a while with family but later moved from the area and were not seen again."

Sarah stopped reading and stood there motionless, as if rooted to the spot. The words that John had spoken to her came flooding back to her as if she was hearing him speak all over again. He knew about a person coming to kill a descendant of a man called Artie Stevens.

The librarian couldn't wait to speak despite Sarah's obvious stunned silence.

"I used to love this story as a child, the miracles and so on. Later, as I got older, I kind of thought that maybe it was just a fairy tale made up to help give people hope during a dark time. But now the story about your patient has triggered my memory and really made me think."

"And my patient's name is John too," announced Sarah.

The librarians jaw dropped.

"Or, at least that's what we call him," said Sarah. "He's a 'John Doe'!"

Harold climbed out of bed and went downstairs where he found Val making breakfast. Jenny was sitting happily at the table swinging her legs and scribbling on a page with a crayon.

"Good morning, Jenny," he said with a smile.

Jenny didn't look up. She was too engrossed in what she was drawing.

"She sure loves her artwork doesn't she?" said Val.

"Yes, I guess so," Harold answered, but he couldn't quite remember whether she really did or not.

He sat down at the table beside her.

"Coffee?" asked Val.

"Yea, sure," he answered, nodding.

Val came over and left the coffee-pot down beside him.

Harold's attention was drawn to the small box of crayons that he hadn't seen before. He picked it up and Val noticed him frowning as he examined it.

"I hope you don't mind but I brought a few things with me for her," he explained.

"No, that's fine," said Harold, putting the crayons in front of Jenny.

"What are you drawing?" he asked looking down to see what Jenny had been working at.

"Look," she said, showing him the page.

"That looks nice," he said, not really understanding what it was that she had drawn.

"See," she announced, "that's uncle and that's mammy and that's daddy."

"Wow!" said Harold, "aren't you a really good artist!"

She nodded happily.

The page was covered with random scribbles, but what else can a person say to a four year-old?

Val sat down on the seat opposite Harold, with a plate of food and a cup of coffee in front of him.

"So," he said to Harold, "have you got plans for today?" he asked, in between mouthfuls of food.

"Another day at the office," said Harold.

"Yes of course. Well, if you like, I could take Jenny down to the park?" said Val.

"Err, are you sure?" asked Harold. "That would actually free up Suzie to go and do some shopping."

"It's no problem," said Val, stuffing another piece of bacon into his mouth.

"Right then," said Harold, "that will be a great help. Thanks."

When he had finished eating, Val got everything ready to go to the park, and, about an hour later, headed out with Jenny securely strapped into her buggy. She was very excited as her dad had given her a bag of stale bread to feed to the ducks. On the way to the park Val stopped a couple of times in order to send text messages. When they got there, he stopped again and undid the straps holding Jenny in her buggy. She got out quickly and immediately ran towards the water.

"Wait, Jenny!" Val called out.

She stopped reluctantly.

When he caught up, he took her by the hand and led her over to the water's edge. He bent down on one knee and started to break the bread inside the bag so that it would be easier for Jenny to use. Jenny stood there, eagerly watching him. Then for a moment, her attention was drawn upwards and she looked up into the clear blue sky.

Suddenly, she blurted out, "Uncle, you need five hundred and fifty dollars."

"What do you mean?" asked Val.

"You will need it," she said turning to look at him.

"What on earth for?" he asked, trying to get more information from her.

Jenny just shrugged her shoulders and said nothing more. Val didn't know how to take it and decided to keep an open mind about what she had said, instead of dismissing her.

Val passed her the bag and she began to throw bits of bread into the water and the ducks quickly came over to them. She watched happily as they gobbled up all the bread that she had thrown into the water. When she had no more to give them, they quacked noisily and then moved off to another part of the pond. Now that the ducks had gone, Val checked the time and then walked Jenny towards a park bench which was back near to the entrance. When they got closer, she saw an ice-cream van and began to pull at his arm, wanting to go over to it.

"Hold on, Jenny," he said as they reached the bench, "we are going to wait here for a while, to meet someone."

"Who?"

"He's a friend of mine and he would like to meet you."

They sat on the bench and waited for five minutes but, by then, Jenny could not wait any longer and Val had to go and buy her an ice-cream. A minute after they returned to the bench, a man showed up. Jenny noticed how rushed he looked. Val introduced him.

"Jenny, this is my friend, Johnson. He works as a gardener at a big mansion."

Jenny smiled up at him.

She sat on the bench swinging her legs and eating her ice-cream while the two men stood and discussed several things, often in whispers so that Jenny could not hear. When her ice-cream was finished, she started to pay more attention to their conversation.

"You have to get them to go," insisted Johnson.

"I know, but I don't know how," replied Val, "I don't even know how to tell them the truth about how they got Jenny."

"Take courage," said Johnson, "for the Lord our God is with you."

Balding was making good time on his journey. He had managed to rent a brand new Ford Focus that only had five hundred miles on the clock. It felt very luxurious compared to his own car. He knew the roads out of the city quite well as years previously he used to take his wife out of the city into the countryside on day trips. He drove south out of Chicago and passed through St Louis. When he reached Memphis, he remembered that, many years before, he had travelled down to this part of the country with his wife. It was not much further to Hope now so he decided to turn off the main road and take in a bit of scenery and reminisce about those old times.

As the day drew on, Balding noticed that he needed to stop for gas. When he saw a sign for the next town, he turned and he headed for it. However, the small town he came to looked like a ghost town, with yellow dirt and sand blowing in off the barren hills. All the shops were open but the windows were all dusted over and the paintwork was faded. He pulled in at the gas station.

Mr Balding walked into the shop and over to the owner who was perched on a stool with his dusty feet up on the counter. He placed a hundred dollars down on the desk to cover the cost of the gas and then retuned outside to fill the tank.

A teenager followed him out to the pumps and offered to fill up the tank for him. Mr Balding nodded his consent and handed the boy a dollar tip.

"Thanks sir," said the teenager and set to work.

He must only be about fourteen, noted Mr Balding.

The teenager had blond hair and it was styled as if someone had cut around a bowl on top of his head.

Balding's stomach was beginning to rumble so he poked his head back around the shop door to talk to the owner.

"Hi," he said, "is there a good place round here where I can eat?"

"Molly's diner has the finest burgers in the whole state, its right across the street there. You'll see the red sign!"

Balding went back outside. There was no sign of the teenager.

That's strange, he thought.

He got into the car, put the key in the ignition and turned it. The car wouldn't start. There was no sound, nothing. He frowned and tried again but nothing happened.

"Come on!" he said annoyed, trying again and again. Just then the owner came out onto the forecourt to see what was going on. Balding jumped out of the car and slammed the door behind him. "Damned rental!" he said aloud, his annoyance mounting.

He approached the shop owner, cursing his luck and the car. Within a few minutes conversation, he discovered three pieces of information. The owner said that he knew nothing about the blonde teenager on the forecourt and also that nothing could be done to repair the car without the rental company's consent, and therefore he would be stuck in this town until further notice. He scratched the back of his head in utter frustration as the stress began to show.

With the help of the owner, he managed to push the car out of the way into a nearby parking lot. Then he walked across the street and rented a room in the motel that was upstairs over Molly's diner. He thought the town was dirty and found that his room was no better. The bed had musty sheets, the walls were stained, there was no en-suite and the smell of grease from the diner below permeated the room. The only things the room had in its favour was the one pure-white pillow free of stains and a Gideon Bible on the bedside locker. As he switched on the TV, he discovered that the only channels available flickered to the extent that watching any programme would be really difficult.

He took the phone out of his pocket and dialled the number on his rental contract papers.

"Hi, Redco car rentals, Sanrio speaking. How may I help you today?" said the person who took the call.

Balding snapped, "My name is Balding. I rented a car from you and the wretched thing has just broken down."

"What's your reference number?" asked Sanrio, disregarding his angry tone.

Balding searched the page and spelled out the reference, "It's D-F-6-9-0-8-7."

"Ok, Mr Balding. Where are you exactly?"

"I'm just off Route 278 in a little town called Warren."

"Can you spell that?"

"W-A-R-R-E-N," said Mr Balding, pronouncing each letter as distinctly as he could.

"Thank you sir," said Sanrio.

"So, how soon can you get me a replacement car?" Balding asked impatiently.

"I have noted the problem and we should have it resolved within forty-eight hours, sir," said Sanrio calmly.

"Forty-eight hours! Are you serious?" said Balding furiously.

Sanrio reacted to Balding's remark saying, "That's our standard response time. We do get many issues resolved within a few hours but our response times are on a case-by-case basis. We will be in touch as soon as possible to let you know."

Mr Balding went silent with both shock and frustration.

"Anything else I can help you with today?" asked Sanrio.

"No!" said Balding abruptly in exasperation.

"Goodbye Mr..."

But Mr Balding had already hung up. With a huge sigh, he gathered his few things and headed downstairs to the diner below.

Mr Smith climbed out of bed and sat on the edge of it. His head felt a bit shaky, probably from the 'few' glasses of whiskey that he drank the night before. In truth, he was taking his time travelling across the country, driving only a couple of hundred miles a day and then stopping in a town or at a motel and taking a break. In a way, he hoped that he would get news that his time of leave was over and that he could return to work. He hoped that this would happen before he ever reached Hope.

That place, he thought to himself, *what a bad memory!*

Recollections of his childhood in Hope began to flash through his mind. He remembered how the small-town attitudes, where everyone seemed to know everything about everybody, had driven him mad. This was especially true because his family had been regarded firstly as outsiders and then as dysfunctional. He stood up and began to pace the room.

"If it weren't for my father," he said out loud and then punched at the wall.

Truth be told, his father's life had been a mess and his actions had dragged the family into tough times. He had come from a rich family but, by the time 'Smith junior' was born, he had already wasted all of his inheritance. There was nothing more for him to get, in spite of his pleading several times with the grandparents. He had been accustomed to fine living all his life and so, when there was no money, debt came quickly on the family. The outcome was that he became a drunk and got very abusive to his wife, venting his self-hatred out on her.

Then, Smith remembered the night that it had all changed. He was fifteen at the time and was awoken by his father coming home shouting and screaming. That in itself was not unusual. However, after a row between his parents erupted, suddenly there was a loud bang. Smith, scared out of his wits, came cautiously downstairs, only to see his father take off in the truck and his mum lying on the floor, bleeding profusely. He instinctively ran to her side before calling for an ambulance. She had been shot.

Soon the whole town had gathered, curious to see what had happened. Thankfully, his mum pulled through; the bullet had passed near her heart, just missing it by an inch. Later that night, his dad's truck was found crashed into a tree. They came and told him that his father was dead. From then on, everyone in town openly said bad things about his father, but Smith couldn't listen to them. Yes, his father had done bad things but he was still his dad. He needed to grieve the loss but all he got at school was rejection, scorn and bullying. At the age of eighteen he had left town promising never to return. His grandparents had left him enough money for college so he took the opportunity to get away.

Years later, he received a letter from a law firm in Hope informing him of an inheritance left for him in his mother's will. She had also passed away. He never went back, not even for her funeral. He never even contacted the law firm back. All he had was the key of the house which he had somehow kept on to through the years.

It's probably in an awful state now, he thought.

Smith went into the bathroom, splashed some water on to his face and then stared long and hard into the mirror. Since he started the journey, he had been letting his personal appearance slip. As he wasn't in work, he decided there was no need to shave and as he wasn't with any friend, or lover, he saw no need to shower either. But now, as he stared at his rugged, tired, 'hung-over face', with a fair length of beard beginning to cover it, he realised something: he was looking far too much like his dad.

I think it's time to get cleaned up, he thought. *And not just my face; I need to sort all this left-over stuff from my past.*

Silas got back to his cabin just before nightfall. The fire that he had left burning had long since gone out but some of the heat from it had remained in the room. It was definitely much warmer in here than outside. He went to the bed and spread out on to it all the things that he had managed to steal from the house he had raided.

I reckon this lot will last me for two or three days, he thought to himself.

He began to wish that he had got more.

"I guess I'll have to go out on the hunt again soon," he said, sighing.

Eager to get the fire going again before dark, he went back out into the forest to find more wood in the undergrowth.

This done, he soon had a fresh fire going and a homemade stew cooking in a pot over it. He had started with water and then added bits and pieces from the things he had stolen, both meat and vegetables. In reality, it would be more like a soup but he was calling it 'stew'. It was basic but, when you are starving with the hunger, there is no point in complaining. The stew would be his one and only meal for the day. He was forcing himself to ration it so that he would have enough left over for the following two days. He was aware that he had to start building up his energy and so, as soon as he had eaten, he some put more wood on the fire and climbed into bed to get a good rest.

But as soon as he fell asleep, dreams came.

"What's his name?" asked a man with a dark menacing voice.

"Silas," was the reply.

"Have they found him yet?" asked the man.

"No, police are saying that he drowned along with the guards."

"And you don't think so?"

"No. That guy has a knack for survival. You'll take the job then?"

"I will, but I want payment up front just in case the man is dead already. My time is money. Ten should do it."

"And you understand that I want him to suffer?"

The man who had spoken picked up an apple, and began to peel it with a knife. With a sinister voice he added, "I will carve him up, cut his skin off and then take photos. You'll be more than happy."

"I want to speak to him before the end."

"No problem."

A bag was thrown on to the desk with money inside it.

As the guy moved from the shadows, Silas could see his face. It was an old friend of his, a guy who used to run with him.

He woke up, covered in sweat.

As the night went on, he had several more dreams. There were no more dreams about his former friend, but instead they were about those who had suffered at his hands, people he'd murdered, assaulted or robbed, all who were victims of his crimes. It was as if he was being taken through their ordeals one by one and, instead of them being victims, he had become the victim and they his persecutors. Silas was glad of the morning when it came. He could not take any more of the dreams. They had begun to break him down.

Linda said goodnight to the children and made herself a cup of coffee. This was the time of the month that she most dreaded – checking the bills. As Sam got paid on a monthly basis, she would sit down once a month and budget, to work out what would be paid out on bills, what had to be bought for school, and any other expense. However, this had become more of a balancing act over the past few months and, as she started, she realised that the month ahead would be no different. She calculated out everything that she would need for the children's living expenses and her own, and then added to that the least amounts she could get away with paying off the bills. What was left over would normally go towards the rent but, this month, she was short, really short by almost two hundred dollars. A cold sweat broke out on her forehead and she went back to double-check everything. As she tried to work it out her coffee, untouched, slowly went cold.
At two in the morning, having checked everything again and again, she began to give up. Her head dropped and tears began to run from her eyes.

There is nothing I can do, she said to herself trying not to panic. *It's not as if I can go out and work. I have the children to look after. Oh God, what am I going to do?*

With that, she burst into tears.

Better to cry it all out now while the children are asleep.

"Oh God," she said. Then she added something she had never dared to say before, "If you really are out there, can you help me? I am really in need here of two hundred dollars, and I've never asked you for anything before!"

She sat quietly for a few minutes wiping her eyes with her sleeve. There was no sound, not one at all. The house was completely silent.

The next day, Linda and the children left the house to go to the store as Wednesday was her usual shopping day. She planned to try to buy the cheaper brands and to find cheaper food to help reduce her spending in order to save a few dollars towards the rent. She stood in silence staring at the various pasta dishes on offer trying to see which one was the cheapest.

"Mommy, look," George said, pulling at her sleeve.

"What is it honey?" she asked.

"It's a ticket," he said waving it in the air.

She took it from his hand and found that it was a lottery receipt. It was muddied a little and its corners were curling up.

I wonder if it's still valid, she thought to herself.

"Thanks George," she said and slipped the ticket into her pocket.

They walked all around the shore as Linda did her very best to compare prices and buy the cheaper coffee, the cheaper bread and the cheaper vegetables. But, when her purchases were all checked at the till, the total amount saved was exactly eight dollars and thirty five cents. She sighed, called the children to her and headed for the door.

"Mommy, mommy," George called to her, "the ticket!"

Something like a light went on inside her brain and she turned back to the girl at the till who was just about to serve the next customer.

"I wonder if you could check this for me?" Linda asked calmly as she handed her the ticket from her pocket.

She watched as the girl scanned the ticket and her eyes opened wide when she saw the girl printing out a payment slip and then opening the till. Scared to ask how much she had won, Linda watched and waited. The girl put down the slip first and then counted out the money in fifty dollar notes. Fifty, then one hundred, then two, then on and on all the way up to seven hundred dollars.

"There you are," said the girl, "congratulations!"

Linda signed the payment slip and took the money. Her hands were shaking. She was almost unable to take in what had just taken place.

With this, she thought, *I can clear a lot of the bills.*

"Mommy, did I win?" George asked excitedly.

"Huh, yes, darling. We won," she beamed. "Yes! We won."

He was jumping up and down with excitement as they left the store.

"Mommy, now that we have the money," said George.

"Yes?" answered Linda.

"The girl that helped me get better, said that when we win the money we have to give it all to her."

Linda stopped in her tracks and stared at him.

"But we can't do that right now George," she said. "Mommy really needs the money,"

"But we have to mommy, we have to," he said with insistence.

Linda was speechless. She was still at a loss trying to process all that was happening.

"There she is, mommy!" George said excitedly and went running down the boardwalk to meet Jenny.

Linda followed quickly, pushing the other two children in the buggy.

She immediately recognised the little girl but not the man who was with her. When she caught up with George he was already busily speaking to the little girl.

"Hi," she said, "I'm Linda. That's George, and these are Jason and Damon."

"Hi, nice to meet you," said the man, "I'm Val, and this is Jenny."

"Are you her dad?" asked Linda.

"No, I'm her uncle," explained Val.

"Oh I see."

"Come on, George, let's go. Say goodbye to your friend."

George turned and looked up at her.

"The money!" he pleaded.

"The money?" enquired Val.

"George found a lottery ticket in the store and we won some money but then he told me that he is supposed to give all of it to Jenny."

At this Jenny spoke, "Uncle, you have to take the money. Remember, I told you."

"What's that?" asked Linda.

"At the park yesterday, Jenny told me that I will need a certain amount of money."

"Oh... listen, I am sure that you are both really great people," said Linda, "but please understand, I really need that money right now."

"I completely understand," said Val, "Come on Jenny, let's go."

They began to walk away but when Linda saw George's eyes she began to realise how much heartbreak and disappointment he was experiencing. She decided that it would be much worse for her son to lose faith in her than for her bank manager to do so.

"Wait!" she called and ran to catch up with Val and Jenny.

She pulled out the money from her pocket, handed it to Val and turned and walked away. But Val followed her and tapped her on the shoulder.

"Wait," he said, "there is too much here. Jenny told me that I would need five hundred and fifty dollars, so here, you take the rest."

He handed her one hundred and fifty dollars and she smiled at him gratefully. Then Val took out his wallet and emptied all the loose change and notes into his hand.

"If I need five-fifty then I don't need this," he said passing her the money.

"Thank you very, very much," she said, almost in tears.

"No, it's you who deserves the thanks," said Val sincerely.

When she turned to her children, George looked up at her and just smiled.

As soon as she got home, she counted up the cash that Val had handed her from his wallet. It came to forty one dollars and sixty-five cents. When she realised that this, plus the hundred and fifty dollars from the lottery and the money she had saved while shopping came to exactly two hundred dollars, a tingling sensation filled her body and she began to cry.

"You answered me, God. I didn't even believe in you but you answered me," she said, trembling.

Then she ran into her bedroom, threw herself on the bed and wept.

Luke approached the border checkpoint. His clothes were looking ragged and he had no identity papers to get into the States but he knew that he wouldn't have anything to worry about. He had been travelling for almost three days to get here and he had managed to get this far without needing money.

He walked on to the bridge. The checkpoint was at the other side.

Even from here he could see soldiers with guns and barricades. It was a menacing sight for any immigrant and it was kept that way for that very reason.

There were a number of lanes for cars and queues of about twenty cars had lined up at each gate, waiting to get through. Over to one side was a pedestrian walkway and this is what he was approaching. As he got closer, he could see two guards on duty inside the bulletproof guardhouse that controlled access through the gate. He knew that this would be no problem because of the help available to him. He got to the guardhouse window.

"Passport please," one of the guards said, looking him over.

Luke just stared blankly at him.

"Pasaporte por favor," the guard repeated, in Spanish this time.

Suddenly, yet not at all surprisingly to Luke, both of the guards clutched at their throats and dropped to the floor. He heard the noise of the gate buzzer, pushed the gate open and walked on through.

"Thank you," he said, smirking.

CHAPTER 5

A FUTURE HOPE

Sarah dried her face as she got out of the shower and then wrapped the large bath towel around her body. When she walked back into the bedroom, she saw that Steve had already left. Sarah had noticed that he had been acting very strangely the last few times that they had been together. She sat back on the bed with a sigh.

Why did he go just like that?

She pondered this for some time, analysing everything that had been said and done the night before. The strangest part was that, at the end of their evening out, when she had invited him in, he seemed to be quite reluctant as if he only came in just so he wouldn't hurt her feelings.

Maybe he is seeing someone else? she thought, *he did seem a bit distant.*

She sighed again, lay back and rolled over on to her side. Just then her phone beeped. She grabbed it. It was a text message from Steve. Half-expecting it to be announcing a break-up she paused, taking a deep breath, and then opened it.

This was going so well, she thought, *How could this happen?*

She began to read the message.

It read, "Sorry for leaving suddenly. Lots of things are going on in my mind at the moment, so I needed some time to think. X"

"Things like what?" she texted back.

She motivated herself to get back up and finish drying herself and her hair whilst waiting for a response, but none came. Then she lay back down on her bed and started thinking through every aspect of their relationship. Eventually she fell asleep again and slept until her alarm clock went off, signalling that it was time to get up for work. She got up but was still feeling very uneasy about the Steve situation. As she ate some breakfast, she began to comfort-eat because of the emotional stress.

However, when she got to work she checked her duty roster and, for a change, she was actually going to be working on John's ward. This cheered her up a bit because she was filled with the information that she had gathered the day before on her day off. She left the nurses' station and walked straight to his room. John was still quite a mysterious character and if it weren't for his rugged smelly beard and his missing teeth, she might have even called him handsome.

"Good morning, John!" she greeted.

He turned to look at her and immediately she could tell that he had been in one of his 'trances'.

"Morning," he said back to her.

"How are you today, John?" she asked.

"Am okay, but..." he said, dropping his head on to his chest.

"What is it?" she asked him, coming closer.

"I know it's difficult for you," he said, "but I need to get out of here within three days."

"John, I've told you already. I can't agree to something like that," she said, scolding him.

He came over to her, gripped her by her elbows with both hands and stared directly into her eyes. What he said next left her absolutely flabbergasted.

"Sarah, you are a nice girl and you have a very kind heart. But, everything you do is seen by my Father. Why did you take Steve into your home last night?"

Sarah was shocked, both by the fact that he knew such information about her and also by the way that he had confronted her.

"John, it's just how the world is," she said, trying to justify herself.

He started to shake his head. At this she tried to pull away but he held on tightly to her.

"Sarah, Sarah, stop!" he exclaimed as she struggled all the more to free herself from his grip.

She panicked.

"HELP, I need help in here," she shouted out.

Within seconds, other members of staff came running. They tackled John to the ground and sedated him.

"Sarah," John whispered, his voice barely audible as he began to lose consciousness. "Sarah, if you help me within three days, Steve will marry you."

On hearing what he said, she ran from the room, found a quiet place and began to cry her eyes out.

Suzie came down the stairs to find that Harold had already gone. She saw that he had left her some coffee in the percolator and was thankful for that much. She poured a cupful for herself and began to drink it, knowing that the day ahead could well be a long one. She had sat down with Harold the night before and had decided to take up the school on their letter of invitation to the open day. She went into the lounge and found Jenny there watching TV.

"Hey, princess. How are you this morning? Did daddy get you your breakfast already?"

Jenny nodded, her eyes still glued to the TV.

"Are you ready for your big day?"

Jenny didn't answer but came over and climbed up on to her lap.

"Mom, what is school like?" she asked.

"It's a place where you can learn how to do things. You can make new friends, and oh, you'll be doing lots of fun stuff. It will be nice, you'll see."

"Stuff like what?" asked Jenny.

"Like drawing pictures, reading books, making things, playing games and singing songs."

"Really!" Jenny said excitedly, her eyes gleaming.

"Yes, it will be great. Now, you can watch those cartoons for a while but then you'll have to get dressed. Okay?"

"Okay mommy," Jenny replied.

Just then, Suzie looked up at the clock.

"Oh no! Look at the time! I'm going to get myself dressed now," said Suzie.

She went upstairs taking her coffee with her. Ten minutes later she returned and helped Jenny into her outfit. Suzie had bought Jenny a new outfit a week ago and had decided to let her wear it for the day. Looking down at Jenny, Suzie couldn't help but remember her own childhood experiences. She had a really good memory and could still remember her first day at school. In particular, she could remember the excitement and the cute little lunch box that she carried.

Suzie opened the door and checked outside, it was a cool day and a breeze was blowing in off the lake. She put a jacket on Jenny and then they set out walking to the school. Harold and Suzie only had one car between them and he had taken it to work. Sometimes he did leave it at home and walk to work instead but not today. The school was not very far from the house and as they got nearer, Suzie could see the grey metal railings that surrounded the school grounds. There were two entrances, a pedestrian one and one reserved for the teachers' cars. Parents always had to park outside the grounds, but in this town where most people walked their children to school, this didn't really matter.

As soon as they entered the grounds, Jenny began to pull at Suzie's arm in excitement, wanting to run up to the entrance. The school itself was a single-storey building. It had been built in the eighties and so it was pretty new as school buildings go. It had a grey slated roof and its walls were painted an off-white colour. As they passed the windows they saw that they were decorated with paintings made by the children that faced outwards. They walked through the open door and were greeted immediately by one of the teachers. She was small, about five-foot-two and quite slim.

"Morning," she smiled, "I'm Miss Grantham."

"Hi. My name is Suzie and this is my daughter Jenny."

The teacher bent down to Jenny's eye level.

"Hi, Jenny. How are you today?"

Jenny took a step closer to her mom and held tight.

"Oh, a little shy I see. Tell me, would you like to see your classroom?" she asked.

Jenny nodded and her grip on Suzie loosened.

Miss Grantham led them down the corridor and into a big bright room. Its walls were painted yellow but the desks and chairs were green and blue and the carpet was bright red. Jenny immediately became more curious and let go of Suzie altogether.

"So, here we are," Miss Grantham said, "every child gets their own desk."

"Which one will be mine?" enquired Jenny.

"We don't know yet. You'll have to wait till you come on your first day," explained the teacher. Turning, she pointed across the room, "Over there is the art equipment, paint, colours, crayons, paper and so on." Then, putting her hand on top of some shelves, she continued, "And over here we have our library but there is an even bigger one in the centre of the school. Do you like books, Jenny?"

Jenny nodded and the teacher smiled again.

The teacher turned to Suzie, she said, "Over here is the play area. We generally allow children to bring some of their own things from home too if they like."

"That's nice," said Suzie.

"Now, Jenny," said the teacher, "why don't you go and explore? I need to talk through a few things with your mom. Okay?"

Jenny nodded and ran off happily, first to the toys and then to the art-paper. She took some crayons, found a table and began to draw.

The teacher led Suzie over to her desk.

"Now, for enrolment, we need to ask for a few details," she said, handing her some forms and explaining they would only require standard information.

"We will need I.D. for yourself and your husband, your full names and address and also Jenny's medical history, showing for example, if she is allergic to anything or takes any medication. We have a policy here that if any student has an allergy to anything then any items that would affect them are banned from the classrooms. At present, food containing peanuts are not allowed. We provide a full list showing all of this before the first day of school and that is why we look for information like this on the open day."

"I understand," said Suzie. Then she added, "Just so you know, Jenny is an adopted child."

"Oh really?" said the teacher, "since she was a baby?"

"No," answered Suzie, "we adopted her several weeks ago. She is still quite affected by the loss of her first parents but my husband and I have noticed that she is settling in to our home now."

"She certainly seems to be quite happy. We will treat her no differently from the other children and all the teachers here are very understanding."

"That's great," responded Suzie.

Then she remembered the forms.

"So, when do the forms need to be returned?"

"As soon as possible really," the teacher said.

"Then, I'll sit down with my husband at the weekend and get them done and drop them in sometime next week."

Miss Grantham nodded her acceptance of the plan. She smiled as she shook Suzie's hand.

"I have my next parent due in a few minutes. Please do feel free to look around the school. Take your time and I'll see you again soon," she said.

Suzie smiled back and then crossed the room to collect Jenny.

M r Smith pulled up at the side of the road, and got out of the car. He stood there for a moment remembering his family home in its former glory. Now, by the looks of it, the place had fallen into serious disrepair. The front door was boarded up, all the windows were either smashed or boarded up and the paint was falling off the walls. He walked up along the front path, now overgrown with grass and other plants. As he stepped on to the porch it creaked under his weight. Some garden furniture sat on the porch which had become severely weather-beaten.

He had expected some disrepair but not this much. As he got to the door, he realised that it was sealed with a padlock and so the key which was in his hand would be no use.

"How am I going to get in now? Damn it," he said out loud.

He returned to the car to think over his next move. He came up with the idea that he might find the lawyer's office in town and the person who had written to him years previously. If he did, then he might be able to locate the paperwork and finalise all of the legal stuff that he should have done years ago. Then perhaps he might get a key to the padlock so that he could access the house properly.

He drove off and down through the town but he couldn't find an office so he stopped and went into a hardware store where he was able to get directions and also purchase a few essential supplies. He bought a hammer and some other tools which he thought might come in handy back at the house. Driving off, with the directions, he found the lawyer's office and parked the car outside.

He walked in and spoke to a secretary at her desk.

"Hi," he said, "I'd like to talk to someone."

"Of course," she answered, "what's your name?"

"Mr Smith," he replied.

"Please take a seat" she said, indicating the waiting area. It was a dreary little room with wooden stained panels on the walls. Smith reckoned that it resembled what you'd expect to see in an office of a Private Investigator in TV programmes back in the 1990's and smirked at the idea.

After about ten minutes, a man came out from one of the offices.

"Hi," the man said, "my name is Harold, please come with me."

Smith followed him into an office which was brightly decorated. It even had a huge window and modern furnishings.

"Please take a seat," the man called Harold instructed.

"Thanks," said Smith.

"How may I help you today, Mr...?"

"Smith."

Harold motioned for him to continue talking and took out a pen and a sheet of paper out to have ready to note down any important details.

"I certainly do hope that you can help me," said Smith, "you see, I live up in Washington and I haven't been back this way in many years. However, when my mother passed away... actually a good while afterwards, I received a letter from this office stating something about a will. I know I should have come sooner, but it was a difficult time for me," he explained.

"I see, and how long ago was that?" Harold asked.

"Too long," replied Smith.

"Have you got that letter with you?" Harold enquired.

"No, sorry."

"Okay then. What was your mother's name?"

"Marjorie Smith and she lived at Becket's Court," stated Smith, "I passed by the house on the way here and it was all boarded up and under lock and key."

"Wait! I think I know the place. Is that on the road out towards the lake, along on the left, with an overgrown garden?"

Smith nodded.

"Yes, that's it."

"I don't remember the particular case though," Harold continued, asking, "can you hang on a few moments while I go and check our files?"

"Sure! Thanks."

Harold got up and left the room while Smith waited patiently. A short time later Harold returned with a brown folder in his hand. He placed it down on the desk as he sat back down.

"Is that it?" asked Smith.

"Yes," said Harold as he opened the file. "It seems like your mother was a very wise lady and had a trust set up to cover the inheritance taxes. Also, it looks like my predecessor, dealt with the case. The last note on the file reads 'Waiting for claimant to return'."

Having read that, Harold began to scratch his head.

"What is it?" asked Smith.

"It's just that, normally, if a claimant doesn't show up within a certain amount of time, most firms like ours usually consider applying for ownership of the property."

"What do you mean?" asked Smith beginning to feel alarmed.

"In new inheritance laws that were passed three years ago, any inheritance not claimed within nine months can become the property of the lawyers involved. Of course, the government takes most of the value of the property by a new tax. The idea was to help lawyers who have been left out of pocket as a result of bringing inheritance cases and cases involving wills to court."

"So then it's not my house after all!" said Smith, his shoulders sagging.

"Hang on, Mr Smith," said Harold quickly, "it seems that our firm never applied for ownership, and, looking at the documents, it seems that my predecessor has already signed a waiver. Obviously we could take it to court but I'm not in a mean mood today," he said, looking up at Smith and grinning.

"All you need to do is sign here," Harold said, pointing to the paperwork and marking the correct place with and 'X'.

Smith leaned over the desk and signed his name. Then Harold returned the page to its place in the file and then turned back to the first page.

"Ok, so let me read this out to you," Harold paused, looking up to make sure he had Smith's attention. Then, he continued the document, "The last will and testament of Marjorie Smith..."

Michelle put the phone down, her body feeling the thrill of her enthusiasm. She had been waiting for a big breakthrough like this, for something that would take her into the league of the great journalists.

This is it, she thought, as she got up and walked towards the editor's office.

The editor was a lump of a man, overweight, with a beer-belly and with a fierce attitude that tended to intimidate all who worked under him. No one went near him on a bad day and, with him, most days were bad days. In fact, he was so often stressed out that there were bets on when he might keel over and die of a heart attack. Currently the pot was over five hundred dollars. The editor had never really liked Michelle, not since her first day when she walked in just after graduating in journalism. Maybe there was something in him that was jealous of her. Not only did she have brains but she also had looks to match. She was the kind of head-turning blond that most guys couldn't help following with their eyes, and indeed their eyes did follow her whenever she strolled through the office. This, to tell the truth, had made things all the more difficult for her, with the guys not taking her seriously and the other girls being jealous of all the attention she was getting. As a result, she had not found even one friend in the whole news station. Settling in to life in Detroit had been quite awkward for her, but that was now two years previously.

Things are about to change, she said to herself as she reached the door of the editor's office.

"Charlie," she said, as she entered.

"Close the door, Chelle," he responded.

She swung around and closed it rather noisily.

"I've got a huge lead, boss!" she announced, excitement in her voice.

As soon as she said the word 'lead' he took his eyes off her and started to fiddle with his papers.

"What is this 'lead'? he asked, in his usual abrupt manner.

"It's about the Tyrell story," she replied.

Now Charlie sat up and gave her his full attention as soon as he heard her say mention 'Tyrell'.

"Did you land an interview with Mr Tyrell's folks?"

"No, I haven't."

"Oh," he said disappointedly, "who have you then? Some ex-floozy of his?"

"No," she said, "not that either. I've got somebody much better."

"Who then?" he asked, wondering who else it could possibly be.

"I have Mr Tyrell himself," she said, her face gleaming.

Charlie stared at her, perplexed.

She continued, "Earlier today, I had a talk with the nephew of a guy who claims to have been there when Luke Tyrell was found, washed up on a beach down in Mexico!"

"In Mexico! You're kidding, right? These people are probably just after money."

I'd best not mention the money right now, thought Michelle, wanting to pick the right time to mention that topic.

Instead she said, "I looked into the story and dug around a bit. I found another guy who gave Luke a lift towards the border," she declared.

"Pffff," sniffed Charlie.

"So, I contacted the local border police to ask if they had come across Luke. They asked me for his details, his height, and hair colour and so on and I told them what I knew. They then told me about a man who fitted the description I had just given them. They said he had managed to escape across the border and that the local police are currently conducting a search for him."

"But that's crazy," responded the editor, still perplexed.

"I know!"

"I mean, it's too crazy to be true," he snapped, back to his usual self.

Michelle stared blankly at him as he declared sarcastically, "I can spot a fake story a mile away and I ain't got the resources for you to go on some wild goose chase that you've probably invented just so you can get a holiday in Mexico."

She stood up and stood by the door. She had a trump card and she used it.

"That's alright boss, maybe Channel Six will have the resources. I think I'll give them a ring and ask."

"Now hold on young lady," said the editor changing his tone to a more conciliatory tone.

"Yes?" she said, raising her eyebrows.

She knew that she had put the ball firmly back in her boss's court.

Johnson arrived at the mansion. He had been employed here as a gardener for almost two years now and found that it was not such a bad place to work. The pastor and his wife didn't pay him a huge wage but it was enough for him to live on in the little town. Besides, he enjoyed the simple life. He remembered how almost ten years back, his mind had suddenly been drawn towards hope. He had suffered depression as a child and was going through the process of renewing his heart and mind after becoming a believer. Around that time, people had kept coming up to him telling him how he needed to find 'hope' and telling him that 'hope' must be in his eyes and heart. Such things had been said to him so many times that it reached a very weird level. Then, one day, he saw a newspaper article about the hospital in Hope and how it was doing great work with its patients. Once he realised there was an actual place called Hope he wanted to move there. However, back then he had been unable to move straight away so he had waited until the right time, which came several years later.

Having been led to move when he got there, doors had opened up for him quickly. The previous gardener at the mansion had just retired and so he had the job secured within days of arriving in Hope. It was here at the house that he had met Barbara, who works at the mansion as the cleaner. Now they were planning a life together and hoped to get married soon and he knew that, when they did, they would have to move away and live elsewhere. That time was had now come. He had many things to organise before they left and so his time as a gardener was coming to an end and he knew it.

Although, for the most part, he had enjoyed his job, he never liked it when the pastor was around. Johnson had a very insightful view of the pastor and his form of 'Christianity'. But then, of course, he knew a lot more about the deception than perhaps the pastor would ever realise. Whenever he saw the pastor, he thought of only one word, 'corruption'. But, at the same time, Johnson had to admit to himself that he must be working at the mansion for some purpose, although up to now he had never really worked out quite what that might be.

He pulled up outside the servant's entrance and set about doing his work. He went to the shed and fetched out the ride-on lawnmower.

This is the last time for me to be cutting the grass, he said to himself.

He did love the garden at the house. It covered a big area and it gave fantastic views of the lake and the surrounding landscape. He had happily spent much of his time working away in peace and frequently in prayer as well. Johnson loved to pray and he had been recently showing his future wife how to persevere in prayer. It had been unfortunate that the two of them had been caught in the act by the pastor. Part of him had wanted to respond by saying, 'Why don't you join us pastor?' but that would have only led to an angry reaction by the pastor.

"The International Church people don't like us 'fanatics' at all," he said aloud, shaking his head.

Johnson had just received confirmation at the weekend that he should go ahead with the plans to marry and move away. Also, after meeting with Val, there was urgency in the atmosphere that they had to respond to. It was certainly time for another meeting of fellow believers. They did not occur as often as any of them would like as the risks of being caught were always high, and any meeting increased those risks. He was curious as to who would turn up this time.

"That's always the joy of it," he said.

Johnson was the organiser for the local area and he always found it amazing how the meetings were protected from people that they didn't want to see turning up. He remembered how only three months before, two men had come to town and asked questions about the 'fanatics' pretending that they wanted to take part in their meetings or to help them in some way. Their cunning was enough to fool some of the people who informed them about an upcoming HSP meeting but, when they didn't show up, everyone knew that they were deceivers. In fact, neither man was ever seen in town again.

The term 'HSP' which they used for their meetings, represented what had attracted Johnson's fascination many years before. The three letters stood for 'Holy Spirit Place'. He had heard stories during his childhood about the underground church in Russia and how believers would never announce where or when to meet but the Holy Spirit would bring them together at the exact right time and place. This had always been something that had baffled his reasoning powers, but, after the true church got labelled 'fanatics', it was a method that he and many others used for their personal protection. Now that he was leaving the area, he knew that a new organiser would have to be found, but that job wasn't for him to worry about. He knew that God would fill that position after he moved on.

After a morning of in depth thinking, and prayer, Johnson went looking for the pastor and found him taking a stroll not far from the house.

"Good afternoon," said Johnson affably.

"Hello," answered the pastor, "what is it?"

"Pastor, I'm afraid that something has come up and I will be moving away from Hope and so, I would like to hand in my notice."

The pastor sighed. He didn't quite know what to say but was more concerned about what his wife might say about it. She very much stressed over such things.

After some thought, he said, "I've always found you to be a hard worker, apart from that incident last week, but I'll not think any more about that. I'll make sure to give you a good reference and a bit of extra cash when you leave to keep you tided over."

"Thank you very much," said Johnson gratefully, "I really appreciate that."

"May I ask what's taking you away?" asked the pastor.

"Family reasons," said Johnson, dodging the real answer.

"I understand and I wish you all the best," said the pastor graciously.

Johnson walked away.

That went better than expected, he thought.

"Thank you Lord!" he said aloud once he was alone.

Linda just sat there on the sofa for hours, staring at the TV that was not even switched on. She had been awoken at four, not by crying children but by a restlessness that she felt within her. Things in her heart had changed. She had come to terms with everything that had happened over the past couple of weeks even the strange things that she had witnessed happening to her children. She had accepted the reality of them taking place, but she was still filled with questions such as how are miracles possible and why did they happen. She pondered why was this happening to her family and, especially, why did God suddenly come on the scene when he had not been around during the tough times when she was a child herself. With all of this going round in her head, she was left restless, yearning for answers and needing someone to talk to about what was going on.

Yesterday after the financial miracle, she had decided to go to the local International Church where she had met a caretaker pastor who looked at her sideways with consternation when she mentioned the word 'miracles'. His reaction, along with the fact that the children were playing up, led her to make her excuses and leave the place. However, the children had calmed down as soon as they were off the premises and the whole experience, therefore, had left her with even more questions.

Why did the children not like that place? Why did the man who is supposed to know about God not have a clue about miracles?

So for hours now she had stared at the TV, lost in thought and sipping on cup after cup of coffee.

George suddenly opened the door and walked into the room. He came over and cuddled up beside her.

"Hey, love, how are you? Did you sleep?" she asked, looking down at him.

He nodded.

"Why are you up, mommy? he asked.

"I got up early because I couldn't sleep, darling," she replied.

"Why?" he continued, looking up at her.

"I just have a lot on my mind," she answered, turning her head to avoid his look.

"Like what, Mommy?"

"Just about... many things," she said, not wanting to be too specific.

"Don't worry, mommy," he said, "I had a dream."

"A dream? What was it about?" she asked, curious to know.

George went on, "We were walking through the park near the hospital. We climbed over a hedge and then a fence but, as it got dark, we saw the light of a fire. We walked towards the light in the middle of the darkness and there we found everyone."

"There we found who?" asked Linda.

"All of the people," said George.

"What people, honey?" asked Linda, more curious than ever.

"The people who have the answers," said George in a matter of fact way.

Linda's mind began to accept the reality of what her son was telling her.

She had no reason not to believe him after everything that had been happening.

Maybe we should go find this place. I suppose if you really search for something, then you will find it.

"George," she said.

"Yes, mom," he responded.

"When are we supposed to go to the place you saw in your dream?"

"In three days," George answered, "when it's nearly dark time!"

CHAPTER 6

GATHERING HOPE

Mr Balding sat quietly staring at the screen of his computer. It was unable to connect to the internet because whatever way the motel had its internet set up, it just refused to let him connect. It was as if something was blocking him from gaining access. He wouldn't mind so much but he had received a notification that on one of the social networks, a new post had been put up saying, 'Meeting, three days, HSP'. The email notification had come through to his computer but he remained unable to open up any website. He had hoped to find comments from other people that might give him some clues as to the source of the message. He had thought long and hard about the letters 'HSP', and what they could possibly refer to and when he had checked back his notes, he had found references to them all over the place. However, after long hours of searching and a lot of thought, his search was still fruitless. Frustrated, he switched off the computer.

"Useless! I hate this place!" he retorted angrily.

To make things even more frustrating for him, he was still stuck in what he called 'this little town in the middle of nowhere' and, despite the car rental company promising a solution in less than forty-eight hours, that time had already expired. He had called them several times, but still no one had made the effort to come and sort out the problem for him.

Never again will I rent from them! he announced to himself.

As a result of all this, he was beginning to think that he would have to spend another night in the town. To add to his problems, his money had also run low. It wasn't that he had financial problems, it was due to the fact that the only ATM in town displayed an 'out of order' sign and a note attached to the machine said that it could not be repaired until after the weekend. He knew he would have to survive on what cash he had in hand and so he couldn't even go out to the local bar for a few drinks. He had even to cut back on meals and so here he was, bored, frustrated, tired and hungry.

He went over and sat on his bed and flicked the TV on. The station was fuzzy and flickering as usual but this time the sound was clear so he turned up the volume. Then something else caught his eye. Right there beside him on the bedside cabinet was a Bible. He picked it up.

I thought these were banned, he thought to himself as he began to examine it.

He opened to read the inside-cover. It read, 'Issued January 1981'. Lower down the page it read, 'Published in 1976'.

"No wonder," he said laughing aloud. "A dump like this place probably hasn't been updated since 1981!"

He let the pages run between his fingers and then stopped them and read what he saw, "But those who drink the water I give will never be thirsty again. It becomes a fresh, bubbling spring within them, giving them eternal life."

"Absolute nonsense," he said, closing the book and throwing it back on to the cabinet.

Then with a sneer, he said, "Living water! Eternal Life! Sounds like there's a well hidden in some cave that I'd have to drink from so that I can live forever, it's no wonder all these fanatics are crazy, believing stuff like that. If I asked this 'God' for help and said, 'Lord I am thirsty. Give me living water,' would I get a reply? No I..."

There was a knock at the door. Mr Balding was surprised but got up and answered it.

"Mr Balding?" asked the man standing at the door.

"Yes?" enquired Balding.

"I'm from the local store and I heard that you were in a bit of a pickle so I brought around some things for you," said the man, rather awkwardly, holding out a brown paper bag.

"Why, thanks!" said Balding, taking the bag. The man then turned and walked away.

Mr Balding shut the door, went back and sat on the edge of the bed and reached inside the bag to start lifting things out. The first thing he found was a bottle of water.

That's weird, he thought, *Maybe I should have asked this God to sort out the rental company as well.*

At that very moment, the phone rang.

He left down the bag and answered it.

"Hi, is that Mr Balding?"

"Yes, that's me."

"It's John Kavanagh here, sir. I'm calling to let you know that we will be dropping off a replacement car for you."

"When?" asked Balding, his heart racing.

"I'm on my way and should get there in about an hour or so."

"That's great! Thank you very much!"

Finally! he thought as he hung up the phone. *This place was starting to get to me.*

He thought about what had just taken place but quickly dismissed it as pure coincidence.

I've seen much bigger ones than that, and none of them prove to me that God exists.

He took the rest of the stuff out of the bag and tucked into the food that the man had brought.

Val walked towards the diner in the centre of town. He wasn't too keen on meeting other believers in such a public place but, when Steve had called him, he had sounded very upset, torn up in fact, and so Val knew that the meeting could not wait. He had not seen Steve for about a year now, not since he had last come to Hope. He remembered how zealous for God the young man had been, and so Val was wondering what might be upsetting him so much. As he walked into the diner, suddenly he got a feeling, a kind of heavenly prompt, that he needed to get back to the house as soon as possible. This put him on edge.

"Would you like to order anything?" a young waitress came and asked him.

"A pot of coffee please," he answered.

The diner was decorated in a 1960's style, but not in a good way.

It's always looked like this, he thought as he looked around.

He had sat down in one of the padded cubicle seats near the rear of the diner. It was about as private a spot as one could get in the place but, even from where he sat, he could still see the front windows and the door.

The waitress returned with his pot of coffee.

"Thanks," he said, smiling.

"Anything else?"

"I am actually waiting on a friend."

"Sure, sure, I'll come back."

Val turned a cup right-way-up and placed it in a saucer and poured himself some coffee. As he looked up he saw that Steve had just arrived so he stood up and greeted him with a hug.

"It's been too long," Val said.

"That's certainly the truth," replied Steve.

Steve took off his jacket and sat down. As soon as he did the waitress came back over to them.

"What can I get you?" she said, looking at Steve.

"Tea and some of your apple pie please," answered Steve, returning the menu card to its holder on the table.

"No problem, I'll be right back," she said.

She walked off, apparently happy that the diner was getting the business.

"So, Steve, it's been a while, the year has gone so quickly! How have you been?" asked Val.

"Yeah, it has been too long," said Steve, "how are things up in Connecticut?"

"Not good at all," sighed Val, "I'm afraid I won't be able to go back there."

"What happened? I thought that the..." Steve paused, looked over his shoulder and then whispered, "I thought that the church there was going really well?"

"It was. But, someone on the inside informed the authorities and now, the believers, they are all gone and the police are probably looking for me. It was horrible! People were gathered up like cattle into cages. It happened in the middle of the night while the others were still sleeping."

"How did you manage to escape?"

"Me? Well I had woken about an hour before they stormed the houses. The Lord asked me to get up and go for a walk. I just wish the others had done the same."

"That's bad news indeed," said Steve.

"Don't worry Steve, God always has a plan."

"Speaking of which, do you remember what you prayed with me for, the last time we met up?"

"Of course," answered Val.

"Well, I think that I have found her," said Steve.

"The future Mrs Steve, eh?" joked Val.

"Yea," said Steve a sigh, "that's for sure!"

Val saw that Steve wanted to have a serious conversation about the matter.

"What is it?" he asked.

"It all began about six months ago when I hit a rough patch. I was absent a lot from work and was just feeling really down so I started spending a bit too much time at the bar here in town. Then, not so long ago, this young lady, a stranger, walked in and we hit it off straightaway. The thing is Val I was at a low point, weak..."

"Go on," prompted Val.

"Let's just say things went too fast too soon," said Steve, his eyes downcast.

"Oh I see."

"Yeah," sighed Steve, "and now the whole thing is in a royal mess. She wants things to be done her way but I've changed direction. I want to live my life in the right way but this has put a rift between us and now I don't know what to do."

"That's a lot to take in. Tell me," Val said, "do you really love her?"

"Yes I do. I love her more than anyone I have ever loved before. I love her so much that I'm willing to walk away from our relationship rather than hurt her by continuing on with things as they are."

"And what does your lady-friend think about what you believe in?"

"I haven't actually discussed it with her. Because I was going through a rough patch when we first met, I never mentioned Jesus at the start, and then I found that I could not go back later and tell her about him. I got stuck in the mess that I created for myself."

The waitress returned with the tea and the pie.

"Thanks," said Steve.

"If you guys need anything else, just let me know," she said.

Both of them smiled up at her and nodded. The waitress walked away, leaving them to talk.

"So Steve, how do you think she might react if you did tell her?" asked Val, returning to the subject.

"My biggest fear is that out of hurt, she might report me as a fanatic," answered Steve.

"I guess that's a possibility, but then there is always a risk when it comes to loving someone."

"Yeah, I see what you mean," said Steve, "it's just that I am undergoing such guilt for my lack of self-control that it makes it hard for me to even consider continuing my relationship with her. But I would also be gutted if I lost her," he added, still dejected.

"Would you be more gutted if you lost your relationship with God?" asked Val.

"Yeah! For sure!" replied Steve.

"Have faith, Steve," Val said. "Everything will come together in God's good time, I know it may seem as if you're walking through a field on a foggy night only to find it has quick-sand in it..."

"You couldn't have put it better," said Steve.

"But there is always a greater plan, one which we all need to submit to," said Val wisely.

"That's right," admitted Steve.

"You know what you have to do, don't you?" asked Val.

"Yeah," muttered Steve, "I will have to let her go and give our relationship back to God. Then whatever happens will be in his hands."

"Exactly," said Val nodding his approval.

Steve stopped talking and began to tuck into his pie. He felt much more at peace now after talking things through with Val.

Suzie waited patiently by the kitchen table. She had just come down stairs after putting Jenny to bed.

"Come on, Harold, turn the TV off" she said, calling him for the third time.

Harold came into the room and sat down beside her.

"I don't know what the hurry is!?" he said looking up at her.

"We've been given a registration form by the school yesterday and today I got a follow-up call from the Department of Education because the teacher that I met had forwarded on our contact details. So now we have to get this form filled in," she explained.

"Okay, okay," said Harold, "I was only trying to watch the end of my fishing program."

"It's a good time to do it now while the house is quiet, and Val is out somewhere," she pointed out.

"Okay, let me see," Harold said, taking the form from her and reading each part through carefully.

"Have you got a pen?" he asked.

"Oh yes, wait," said Suzie as she got up to fetch a biro from the drawer.

"Thanks."

Harold began to fill out each part of the form that was relevant to him, his name, address, phone number, job details, and his social security number.

"Here," he said, "now you have to fill out your side. Just copy what I've done on the left. Your details go on the right," he explained.

"Ok," she said, scratching her head and taking the pen and form from Harold. She was not that good at filling out forms and had often needed Harold to help her out because in the past she had sometimes made a mess of forms. Harold supervised her patiently.

"Done!" she said finally.

"Great," he said, taking the form back from her. He made one last check over her details.

"Looks good. Now we just need to fill in Jenny's details."

"I've got her documents here," said Suzie handing him the birth certificate showing the name Jenny Hart.

"Thanks," he said, but suddenly he stopped and stared at it.

"This has us down as her parents," he noted.

"I know," answered Suzie, "We are her parents!"

"Yes, but shouldn't her birth parents be on it instead?" he said.

"I don't know. Maybe the adoption agency changed the details so that she will be seen as our child?"

"But that makes no sense. Jenny already knows that we are not her real parents."

They stared blankly at each other. Then they began to trawl through all the paperwork that they had received from the adoption agency, the letters, documents and certificates. The more they looked the more they got confused. None of the information that they needed for the school was there.

"This is really weird," Harold stated.

"It must be above board, it must be..." he said frowning. "But there's something not adding up here."

Harold wondered why he had not noticed the issue before.

"What do we do now?" asked Suzie.

"I guess we should phone the adoption agency and ask them," answered Harold.

"I don't know," said Suzie. "What if it's all a mistake and they take Jenny away from us?"

"Look, I'm sure that it's alright. Let's just call them."

Harold went and picked the landline phone from the kitchen wall. It had one of those old-fashioned stretch leads so he took the phone, sat back down and instead of dialling the number that was on the letter he looked back through some of the documents and found an emergency phone number which was on call twenty-four hours a day.

As Harold began to dial the number, he looked at Suzie and said, "They might not be able to sort this out till the morning when the office opens, but I'm sure..."

"Hello," said a voice, "This is the adoption helpline. Shirley speaking. How can I help?"

"Hi, could I speak to..." he began.

The phone line suddenly went dead.

Harold looked up and saw that Val was now standing in the kitchen and his hand was on the phone's base unit. He had cancelled the call.

"Val, why did you do that? I was going to make enquiries with the adoption agency!"

"I know," answered Val.

Suzie and Harold looked at each other, totally taken aback by what he had just said.

"I have been looking for a good time to tell you something," said Val, "I guess that time is now."

"What do you mean?" asked Harold nervously, his voice shaking.

"Yes," said Val, "there's something important I need to tell you, something about Jenny..."

Linda quickly finished changing Damon's diaper. The phone was ringing and she made a dash to answer it but didn't reach it in time. She stood there looking at the number listed on the Caller I.D. wondering who it could be. She was sure that she did not recognise it.

I hope Sam is ok, was the first thought that flashed across her mind but before she could even process the thought, the phone rang again.

"Hello," she said, picking up the handset.

There was no reply but she could hear a crackling sound on the line.

"Hello? Hello?"

"H-lo," a voice said.

"I can't quite hear you, hello?"

"Hi, it's me, Sam," she heard her partner say as his voice became clearer.

"Oh, thank God! I can hear you clearly now."

"I thought you might have gone out," said Sam.

"No, I was changing Damon," she explained.

"Ah," said Sam, happy with her answer.

"How are you? Why have you not called me in days?" asked Linda.

"Listen, there's an awful lot to tell you and I can only make a quick call at the moment. The gist of it all is this: something has happened and I am on my way home," he said.

"On your way home? When will that be?" asked Linda, taken by surprise.

"Today. In fact, I'm on the coach from Denver right now," said Sam.

"Denver!" gasped Linda trying to take on board what he was saying.

"What's up?" she asked.

"It's a long story," was all he said.

"Oh..."

"Listen I reckon I'll arrive in about twelve-thirty," he said.

"This afternoon?"

"Yes. Listen, I have to go. Will you be able to come and meet me at the coach depot?"

"Of course."

"Thanks! See you soon. Love you!"

"You too, Sam."

Linda paused for a moment still trying to process the news.

I wonder what has happened and how is it possible for him to come home at such short notice, she wondered.

Then she went into the lounge, took the remote from George and turned down the volume of the TV.

"Guess what, boys..."

George rubbed his eyes and looked at her. It was only eight in the morning and he wasn't quite fully awake yet.

"Your dad is coming home today!" she said excitedly.

George and Jason jumped for joy but Damon sat there staring at them as he was still too young to understand.

Linda looked around and realised that the whole house was in a mess. Straightaway, she got stuck into tidying it. She gathered up the laundry and put it in the wash. Then she hoovered the floors and washed them. She cleaned the bathroom, and put fresh sheets on the beds. After that she emptied the washing-machine and hung the clothes out to dry. While she was doing all this, both George and Jason kept asking her when their dad would arrive. In the end, she began to regret having told them so early.

After the house was cleaned, she left the children watching the TV and took a quick shower and got dressed, making sure to look a bit nicer than usual.

It's not every day that your man comes home from the frontline, she thought to herself as she sat down in front of her vanity mirror to start putting on her make-up.

Then, with everything ready, she checked the time again. It was already ten past twelve.

"Come on children," she called. "Get your jackets and let's go."

They immediately came running and she said to herself that it must be the quickest they had ever obeyed her. George and Jason ran to the door and waited there while Linda sat down with Damon and put his little jacket on and placed him into his buggy.

"Here we go," she said, just as excited as her children were.

They walked briskly down town to the coach depot. It was not a big station really, just a metal-framed shelter for people to stand in. They arrived just in time, half twelve, but the coach had not arrived in yet so they stood watching the road and waiting.

Five minutes later, Linda caught sight of the coach as it came down Main Street and stopped with a hiss from the airbrakes. Its suspension then dropped down so that the bottom step of the bus would be level with the boardwalk. By now, Linda's heart was thumping with anticipation. She remembered back to the last time that she had seen Sam. He had left at night after the children had gone to bed so that it would not upset them but it had still upset them when, the next morning, they woke and found that he was gone. Other than that it had been a nice goodbye but she had cried and cried after he left. She had been overcome with emotion and also the fear about her man never coming back home safely. But here he was now, safe and sound.

"Thank you God for..." Linda stopped praying as soon as she saw Sam. Something was wrong.

As Sam stepped off the bus, Linda realised that he was not in good condition. He looked rough. He was unshaven wearing ragged clothes instead of a uniform. When he saw her, a hint of a smile appeared on his face but even the children stopped in their tracks and stood staring at their dad as he walked towards them.

"Come on, children," Linda said, trying to encourage them, "go and greet your dad."

At that they ran to him. He knelt on one knee and hugged each of them tightly in turn.

Mr Smith had spent the night in a local guest house, but came back to his family home first thing in the morning to start working on it so that he would not have to pay for another night's stay. He turned the key that he had been given in the padlock; the lock was rusty but eventually he got it open. Then he used his door-key to open the lock on the front door and it swung open.

As he stood in the doorway, a breeze swept in past him, gathered up the dust off the floor into the air and spread it like a cloud. He looked around. The only light getting into the house was coming through the open doorway. He reached behind the door for the light switch and pressed it but nothing happened. So he returned to the car and got out the things he had bought the day before. Taking the hammer and a screwdriver, he proceeded to remove the boards that had been nailed up to cover the windows. To reach the upstairs windows, he had to walk up through the house with one hand covering his mouth and nose to protect him from the dust. Once upstairs, he climbed out on to the balcony, walked along it and began to free the windows.

Just then, a truck pulled up on the drive below.

"Ah, the rubbish skip I ordered," he said, looking down.

The driver got out of the cab and approached the front door.

"Just leave it there, in front of the door," Mr Smith shouted down to him and he then proceeded to unload the rubbish skip from the back of the truck.

Mr Smith pulled off the last board and headed back through the house, down to where the driver was standing.

"Could you sign this?" the driver asked, handing him a duplicate invoice-book. Mr Smith put his 'squiggle' in the appropriate place and the driver handed him the top copy.

"Just give us a call when it's full," he said as he turned to leave.

"Will do," answered Mr Smith

He watched as the driver walked over to the door of his truck."

"Hey," Mr Smith shouted.

"Yeah?"

"Have you got any face-masks by any chance?" Mr Smith asked, coming over to the driver.

The driver climbed inside the cab and came back out.

"You're in luck!"

"Thanks! How much do I owe you?"

"Nothing, just take 'em."

"Thanks! By the way, what's your name?"

"It's Steve."

"Thanks, Steve."

When the truck had gone, Mr Smith took a mask out of the pack and placed it over his face. Then he went into the kitchen and filled a spray-bottle with water and began to spray all the floors inside the house. As he got to each window he opened it to allow fresh air to circulate. Once all the dust was dampened down, he began to sweep and then, finally, to mop the floors in each room. Even though he had been wearing a mask, when he had finished and took it off he could feel the after-effects of breathing in a lot of dust. The mask itself was all clogged up.

With all that done, he began to clear out junk from the house into the skip but, because it was beginning to get dark so he concentrated on the living areas: the kitchen, the lounge, the bathroom and what had once been his bedroom. When he had finished, he ventured down into the basement and replaced some of the fuses. This restored power to the house and the lights came on, just in time before complete darkness fell. He went out again and brought in his clothes from his car and then began to cook himself a basic meal.

There's so much to do here. This will take me a week to clear everything out. It has to be done though if I want to sell it, he thought to himself.

After eating the food that he had made, he went up to his old bedroom and took off the old sheets that were still on the bed.

Ugh I'll have to chuck these ones out, he thought as he looked at all the stains on the covers that had been left on his bed.

A REMNANT HOPE

However, when he started to strip the bed, something dropped on to the floor that caught his attention. It was an envelope. He picked it up. The words on it read 'To my darling son'. He froze not knowing what to think or do next. He placed it gently on his bedside locker for the time being and continued getting the bed ready and rolled out the sleeping bag that he had brought with him from the city. Then he sat down on the edge of it, opened the envelope and read aloud the letter that had been inside.

"Dear son, I know that I have not been a good mother to you but I have decided to write this letter to you in the hope that one day you may read it and be able to forgive me. The truth is that my life was messed up before you ever came along, even back in my childhood. And though there is no excuse for my behaviour, I want you to understand that I have always loved you. However, in these last few months, I have experienced something amazing which I hope and pray one day you may also experience too. I have been set free from all the hurt that was done to me and, as I write this, I can honestly say that I am happy and at peace, all except for one thing – that you are gone out of my life. There is not one day that I don't miss you and pray for you. I don't know if I will ever get to see you before the day I die but know this, I love you very much and I am proud of your ability to maintain a good life..."

"Good life! Messed up life, you mean, thanks to you and dad," said Smith with a vicious tone in his voice.

He continued reading.

"...But know this son, everyone in this life has to one day stop and think about their life, about all the things that they have done to hurt people, and about the things that people have done to hurt them. They have to stop and consider if there is a way to be set free from all of that. I can honestly say that I have been set free! I miss you terribly but I am at peace, trusting in a promise that a man said to me last week - that you too, would come to know the Truth and be set free. I had never met this man before, nor will I be likely to ever see him again as he moves around like the wind, without knowing which way it will blow. It was this man who introduced to me to another man called Johnson. Over the last few months, Johnson has really helped me. If you ever meet him, I ask that you would listen to him for he is a man of great wisdom and will help you too. I leave all I have in this world to you and I beg of you to live a better life than I ever did. With all my love, mom."

Mr Smith sighed. All his life, he had wanted to hear words like these. Never had he heard from his mother's lips that she loved him and he had longed for her to say those words all through his childhood.

"Cowardly woman!" he said retorted then broke into tears.

He had until now, always refused to grieve the loss of his mother having seen her as unloving.

After several minutes, he steadied his nerves and began to think over all the stuff she had said about the truth and about living a good life. He thought again about Lisa and about how messed up things were with his job and with his feelings of hurt and resentment towards her. He knew in his heart that he was still in love with her despite her being a married woman, but it was just a big mess. He tried to imagine what it would be like to be free of all of that hurt and confusion but he couldn't understand how such a thing could ever be possible, especially in his case.

Michelle followed the directions exactly and arrived at her destination, San Fernando on the Mexican coast. She had managed to catch a flight out of Detroit. Thankfully, the commercial airlines had begun operating again as the risk of a terror threat had been downgraded. So she flew into San Antonio airport where she rented a car and drove over the Mexican border, and on to the town where she hoped to meet the man who had found Luke on the beach.

All the way down she had thought about the possibility of meeting Luke somewhere during her journey and what that might be like. She thought about questions she would ask him such as, *'How did you come to survive?', 'What happened on the plane?'*, and other questions like them. It was a long-shot anyways but she knew that, having got financial backing from her boss to do some chasing she could now follow his trail across the country.

She turned left, following the instructions on her piece of paper. By car, San Fernando was only an hour and a half from the border and it seemed fairly quiet despite its notorious reputation for smuggling. She pulled in outside a house.

"This must be number thirty-four," she said, looking at the doorframe for a number. She was right.

She grabbed her bag and got out of the car and knocked at the door.

A young man in his twenties wearing shorts and a vest opened the door.

"Qué deseas?"

"Hola, mi nombre es Michelle. From Channel Seven," she said, speaking basic Spanish and mixing it with English to fill in the gaps.

"Ah yes, Michelle, I am Santiago. Please come in."

Michelle was glad to hear that he could speak English.

Santiago led her down the hallway and into the kitchen.

"This is my uncle," he said, tapping his uncle on the leg to wake him up.

His uncle was an elderly looking man with a grey moustache and a balding head.

"Tío, el periodista está aquí."

Michelle pulled out a chair and sat down. Folding her bag she held it under her arms on her lap. She listened carefully as Santiago translated what the old man was saying as he told the story of how he had seen Luke. He said that Luke had actually been found by others first, but he had heard the commotion and gone to take a look at the strange man lying on the beach. It was not until later, while watching the news on an American TV network, that he saw Luke's face and recognised him. However incredible the story seemed, Michelle could tell by the uncle's expression that he was telling the truth. As he spoke he also portrayed a fear of Luke and Michelle picked up on it, although she couldn't work out why.

After the uncle had finished talking, Santiago ushered her towards the door but, as he got to the door, he suddenly put his back against it, blocking her exit.

"Have you got the money you promised?" he whispered.

"Yes I do," she said.

Reaching into her purse, she pulled out an envelope and said, "Here!"

He opened it up and counted the notes inside.

"What about..." she began to ask, Santiago stared back at her but she persisted, "what about the other people who also saw Luke?"

At this, he stepped aside and opened the door for her. She walked out into the sunlight.

"They are all dead, lady," he said firmly, "every one of them."

"How?"

"You tell me, you're the reporter!" he said with a shrug of his shoulders. Then he slammed the door in her face.

Harold and Suzie could hardly believe their ears as they listened to what Val was telling them. It was amazing, not just to hear the truth about Jenny, but to understand how Val and his 'group' had put together such a scheme. It was almost perfect.

"I'm sorry, Val," said Harold, "but I think you will need to start again from the beginning because all this is hard for us to follow. I don't really understand. I mean, why did you do all of this?"

"Okay," said Val.

He sat down on a chair, realising the conversation would be a little more time-consuming than he wanted it to be.

I have to get them to go! he thought, reminding himself of the end goal.

Then he continued.

"Jenny's mother was three months pregnant when she had a troubling dream that she couldn't understand. She went to John, a friend of ours, who has a prophetic gift."

"What does 'prophetic' mean?" asked Suzie, interrupting.

"Oh, right! Err! 'Prophetic' means being able to understand certain things like dreams and visions. It can also make a person able to see into the past or into the future. It's quite diverse actually."

"Oh okay. Carry on," she prompted.

"So Jenny's mother visited John and he informed her that the daughter whom she was expecting was going to be a special person, the first of a whole new generation. Of course, Jenny's parents were totally surprised to hear this, especially when they had not even found out what the sex of the baby was yet."

"That's what 'prophetic' is, is it?" asked Harold.

"Yeah, you got it. But he also told them very specific instructions about how they should raise her and protect her. One very specific thing was that they were not, under any circumstances, to register Jenny for anything. Neither were they to register the pregnancy, nor to register the baby when she was born. They were not to register her for immunisations and, when she got older, not to register her for school. She was not to be registered for any reason."

"I don't understand," said Harold, "what was wrong about registering her?"

"Back then, none of us had any idea either but, we all trusted John so Jenny's parents decided to follow his instructions. They went into hiding up near Connecticut, Jenny's mom, Carol, had to hide her pregnancy. Keeping the pregnancy secret was very difficult for the couple, not being able to celebrate such an occasion in the usual way. The birth was a very difficult one too. We had located a retired lady who used to be a midwife and she came to help to deliver Jenny. But it was a long labour and, there was no medication available for Carol. Yet, the minute Carol laid eyes on Jenny's face, it was as if all of that pain had never happened. There before them was a beautiful baby girl, staring up at them. They both cried, knowing that she was a special baby, a baby born with a purpose."

"What was the purpose?" Harold and Suzie asked together.

"To be honest, we don't quite know. But since Jenny's birth there have been another eleven babies born in the same manner, all of them not registered. We do however issue them with a fake birth certificate. This is why the one you have for her has her name as Jenny Hart, when in fact her birth name was Jenny Stevens. All of them are kept in hiding and, like Jenny, are growing up. The special things that I see in Jenny, I also see in them. They are fearless. They are miraculous. They are brave and they will certainly need to be. I am a firm believer that when times of trouble come, God prepares a way for us to get through. He prepares a remnant who will endure."

"So you're implying that something bad is about to happen. To what? The country? The earth?"

By now, both Harold and Suzie were fascinated with what Val was telling them. Val looked at them and smiled at their innocence.

"Harold, Suzie, it's already begun, and it will carry on and get worse."

"What has?"

"Take Jenny, for example. Her parents, as I said, made many sacrifices. One of these was hiding away from their family and their old friends. They would only allow Jenny to see people from our group so that she would remain hidden and protected. That's the reason why they moved to Connecticut. It was because of a church that had been established there. However, one day, a member of Carol's family found them. He had tracked them down apparently out of concern, but, in doing so, he managed to discover Jenny's existence. There was nothing they could do but greet him and appear to be normal and then try to sort out the problem later. They begged him to stay with them for a few days so that they could explain things and keep everything secret but he refused. So, they had no choice but to tell him straight-out what was happening. The man seemed to accept it. Yet, once he was out of their company and away from the house, he went straight to the police and reported them. That was the beginning of the end."

"The police? So they came to take Jenny away?" asked Harold.

Val shook his head. Then he went on. "No! They came to kill her," he replied.

Suzie gasped.

"I had been awoken at twelve at night by my phone ringing," recalled Val, "it was Carol. She asked me to come over immediately and, when I did, she placed Jenny into my arms and told me to take her to my home saying that they would follow once they had gathered a few belongings. I didn't live far from them, only around the corner. I had just got home and into the living room when I heard the gun shots. That was how Carol and her husband died. They were shot."

"Then what?" asked Suzie.

"When the authorities got wind of our scheme, though at the time they only knew about Jenny, they wanted to shut it down immediately in case the idea fell into the hands of people they termed 'radicals'."

"But you people are 'radicals', aren't you?" said Harold.

"Yes, but these days the word 'radical' is used as if it's a bad thing to be one. Back in the 1970s, however, it was a cool thing to be a radical."

Then Suzie, suddenly realising the implications of what Val was telling them, said, "Then, in that case, all the adoption papers are..."

"Fake," said Val, finishing the sentence for her.

Suzie's face began to show fear.

"Then Jenny is not our daughter after all?" she said, her eyes filling with tears.

"She is your daughter, that is if you still want her..." answered Val.

"Of course we do, but..."

"Listen!" said Val, "we in the group chose you to become Jenny's new parents. It was a unanimous decision but being her parents means that you need to have documents that are good enough to convince the people who will read them. But they have been falsified and the information in them isn't true. But pieces of paper mean nothing anyway. What will Jenny look for when she grows up? She won't be asking you for pieces of paper, will she?"

"But what about school? Jenny needs an education," Suzie declared.

"She will have to be home-schooled. Our group can help out with that where we can, but these days it's a dangerous business being 'radicals' as you called us. It can easily become death by association."

Harold and Suzie looked at each other. Val could see that they would not give up on Jenny no matter what.

"Who was it that brought Jenny to us then?"

"A friend of mine, one of the group. She actually does work for an adoption agency and so she knew the process involved and was able to produce false documents."

"And the story of Jenny being found next to her dead parents?"

Val sighed.

"At first, I didn't really realise what had happened and I couldn't leave Jenny alone, so..."

"You went back!" said Suzie, stunned.

"Yes, I went back. The killers had already left. The normal police, of course, were waiting for a phone call from the public. I found the door left open, and then I saw them lying there. Sadly, Jenny, saw them too but I immediately whisked her away. Thankfully, they hadn't left anyone behind to watch the house. I kicked myself later when I realised how stupid I had been. So, ever since then, I have taken every precaution..."

Harold interrupted him.

"It's not that we regret having Jenny here with us, but why did you choose us to bring her up? What I mean is, aren't you more than capable to look after her by yourself?"

"Good question. There were a few reasons. Firstly, because the authorities would find it more difficult to locate Jenny if she was moved far away from Connecticut. Secondly, because it was our understanding that Jenny actually has family links to this area and to the town of Hope. We also have a secret church here in Hope and so support from other people would therefore be possible. Lastly, I've always known that you two wanted children but couldn't."

Harold looked his brother in the eye and smiled.

"Wait a minute," said Suzie, changing the subject.

"How come we were asked to register her for school?"

"What?" said Val. It was now his turn to be shocked.

"Yes. We received a letter, and a phone call. We even took her down to see the local school."

"When was this?" asked Val, immediately alarmed.

"We took her to the school yesterday. I think the letter came about a week ago?"

"Have you still got it?" Val asked with urgency.

Suzie nodded, and got up and fetched it from the papers stacked next to the fridge.

"Here," she said as she handed it to him.

Val looked down through the letter.

"It looks like a generic letter as there is no mention of Jenny's name on it," Val noted, feeling relieved.

Suzie and Harold came behind him and looked over his shoulder at the letter.

"Then, perhaps it's just an open invitation that they send out to the whole town," suggested Harold.

"Or perhaps, they were looking for Jenny in the area and did this see if they'd get a response! Damn it! I should have thought of this!" said Val, as he thumped his hand down on the table.

Harold and Suzie stared at him blankly.

"There is no time to lose," said Val. "You must pack all your things immediately."

"What? Why?" said Harold, asking two questions in one breath.

"Listen," said Val, grabbing Harold by the shoulders, "nobody 'official' knows that Jenny is here and whoever you met at the school whoever it was who talked to you on the phone, has probably already reported Jenny to the authorities!"

They both gasped, and stood staring wide-eyed at Val.

"Quickly now," he ordered. "We have to go!"

Far above the earth, an object flew quietly along as it came in from outer space and passed through the solar system. It was rock, hard like most rocks usually are. Suddenly out of nowhere, another rock shot across its path and the two of them collided. The resulting explosion sent pieces of debris hurtling out across the solar system.

CHAPTER 7

HOPE REVEALED

Sarah walked out along a lane that led to the lake. She had not come this way before but somehow she knew the directions that she had to take. Sarah continued to follow the lane until a gap appeared in the hedge. She paused momentarily and glanced at her watch.

It's nine already, she noted.

In her heart she felt an excitement about what was in there, hidden in the forest. So, in through the gap in the hedge she went. The forest was dense but under her feet was a soft layer of undergrowth which thickened wherever the trees thinned. As she walked along, the ground rose slightly before dipping down. She walked straight on, taking care not to trip over the roots of the trees. Inside the forest there was an eerie silence, but she wasn't afraid. She felt drawn, called to the place that she was walking to.

A REMNANT HOPE

After coming to a small stream, she stepped over it to the other side and walked up another incline and then down into a ravine. It wound its way along, filled with brambles higher than her head and so she bent down to walk along under them. At the other side, she climbed up out of the ravine and then she saw a light ahead, a light that was shining brightly in the darkness. She started to walk towards it and, as she got nearer, she could hear people talking although she could not make out what they were saying. She stopped at the edge of the trees, still hidden by the branches, and looked out at the group of people who were gathered. Among them she spotted Steve. He was just standing there, staring at the fire. Her heart jumped. She yearned for his embrace.

Then a man suddenly stepped up to her and looked her in the eye. She felt no fear whatsoever because, in his eyes, she found no anger, only love and acceptance. The man was dressed completely in white.

"My dear, you must come and meet us all tomorrow. You know what time. You know who is going to be here."

She nodded.

"And you must set John free."

She gasped in surprise. The man nodded to reconfirm it to her, and then said, "Now my dear wake up. It's time for you to go to work."

With that, Sarah sat up in bed, panting after what she had just seen and heard. All over her body she felt a tingling that only went away very slowly.

"What the hell?" she said out loud.

Her alarm suddenly sounded so she quickly got up, hurriedly got herself ready and then went off to work. Still trying to process the dream, she began to even question her own sanity.

Was it something that I dreamed merely because John told me that I would be the one to set him free? Or, was it just about Steve because I miss him so much? Anyway, who was that strange man in white with those strange eyes?

Her thoughts raced as she went over these questions again and again.

She arrived at work before her shift was due to begin, went to the canteen and got herself a coffee and then sat down at one of the tables in an attempt to calm herself down. Strangely, instead, her thoughts started to think of ways that she could help John escape.

If I drop my keys, he could get them, open the doors and get out. No, no, someone might see him and bring him back. Maybe if I take him outside for a walk in the garden and then just let him run off. They might ask me why he was not strapped in, but I can explain that there were no problems any other time when he wasn't strapped in. No, no! What am I thinking? I can't do this. I could get fired.

She finished her coffee and headed up to the ward to begin her shift. First she went and checked with the head nurse to see if any new patients had come in but none had done so. So she went about her daily duties which by now had become routine and mundane. Sometimes she actually wished that she had chosen a different job but, for the rest of the time, she just got on with things. Soon she came to John's room. She braced herself for what he might say to her.

"Good morning, John," she said as she entered.

"Ah, there you are! It's almost time, isn't it?" said John as soon as he saw her.

"Time for what?" she asked.

I knew that he'd know that I've been thinking about letting him out, she remarked to herself.

"You should realise by now that I know things," said John.

"Oh yeah? Like what?" she retorted, almost sarcastically.

"In a dream, you saw Steve standing at a fire in the forest. And you saw how to get there."

"John, I don't know what you're talking about," she lied, turning her face away from his gaze.

"Yes, you do," John continued, "and you also saw the man in white, didn't you?"

Forgetting the lie, she swung around.

"Who is he?" she asked swiftly.

In answer, John said, "Sarah, you will have to go there to find out. But, I also have to be there. It's absolutely vital because I have to give the people an important message."

There was a pleading in his voice as he spoke.

"John, I can't," stated Sarah. "It's not possible."

"You can do it. Of course you can."

"But how do I know if this is even real, the dream, Steve, the whole thing?"

"Have faith, Sarah!"

"In what?"

"Have faith in the words I have told you. Don't the things I tell you happen as I say they will?"

"Yes, they do."

"Am I not able to tell you things that no one else knows?"

"Yes," she nodded, "you can."

"Then trust me," he said warmly, looking deep into her eyes. He knew that she was destined to let him out but he also knew that he must say the right words to encourage her.

There was a long silence.

"Okay," she said finally.

John smiled at her.

"But if I get caught, I'll kill you! I'll be back in an hour with a wheel chair," she said quietly.

John nodded. He knew that she would keep her word.

"Everything will work out, you'll see," said John taking her by the hand and holding it tightly.

Linda had endured a full day and night of silence. Ever since Sam returned home he had just sat on the sofa, he wouldn't talk, not even to the children, and would only nod or shake his head in response to any question.

There's something terribly wrong, I know it, she kept saying to herself.

Another evening passed and Linda had finished putting the children to bed. George had asked her what was wrong with his daddy and she, faking a smile, told him that everything was fine and that his daddy was just tired.

When she came back downstairs she went to the fridge, took out a couple of beers that had been cooling all day and brought them in to Sam. Then she sat down on the sofa next to him.

"Sam, I'm glad to have you back," she said, taking him by the arm.

He took a beer from her, opened it, looked at the label in silence and then took a sip.

"Sam," she said, touching his hand, "please tell me what has happened to you."

Sam didn't respond. He just stared blankly at the floor.

She decided to try again and to speak more firmly this time.

"You need to talk to someone," she said. "Go and look at yourself in the mirror and see how you look. Even the children can see that whatever is wrong is eating you up inside. Come on, Sam, please tell me because I'm really worried about you."

As she said this, she stroked his jaw with her hand and then gently turned his head so that their eyes made contact.

At last Sam began to talk.

"You wouldn't believe me if I told you," he said, his voice a mere whisper.

"Sam, try me," she said, encouraged that he was at least saying something.

"No, I don't think I can," Sam replied.

"No matter what it is Sam, just get it out. Come on, tell me," Linda replied.

"Okay." He gave a big sigh and took another drink from the bottle in his hand.

He drew a deep breath and began to tell his story.

"It happened about a week ago, just after our fight. There had been rumours all around the camp that the fighting in our area was over. It was even said that we had won and that maybe even the whole war had been won. But it was not official. In fact, staff neither confirmed the rumours nor did they do anything to stop them."

Sam paused, his eyes becoming watery.

"However, the next day half the camp was sent out on what we were told was a 'routine mission'. On the way, we were ordered to put on our gas masks. Again, it was just the routine. But, when we got to where we were sent, we saw that a huge scale operation was underway. There were soldiers from other camps using all sorts of equipment. I certainly couldn't understand what was happening until we went across to the other side of the town. As we drove through the town, I felt that the town was too quiet, haunted even. Then I found out why. On the other side of town they were using diggers and other machinery to dig out deep trenches. Then I saw them, heaps and heaps of dead bodies waiting to be buried."

"Dead bodies!" gasped Linda, aghast.

"Yes, not just a few but thousands upon thousands of dead bodies, all piled into heaps."

"We were ordered to join the other soldiers who were already carrying the dead bodies and throwing them into the trenches. One of my friends and I carried at least thirty bodies of both men and women and threw them into a trench. As we removed them from the heaps, other soldiers were arriving, bringing more bodies out from the houses. I was so overcome. Everyone was..."

Sam paused again taking a deep breath. Then he continued.

"Then I saw the body of a little boy, about Damon's age, in amongst all the others. Beside him lay other children, loads of them. I went up to the commanding officer and asked him what was going on. I asked him who these people were and why there were dead children. He wouldn't answer my questions. Instead, he kept ordering me to stand down. In the end, I snapped and I lashed out at him. It was foolish but I wasn't the only person affected. Other solders had even taken off their gas-masks and were getting sick."

"What had happened to the people?" asked Linda, still in shock, "Why had they died?"

"I still don't know. I really don't. But after the incident with the commanding officer, I was taken away, as were some of the others too. The next thing I knew I was back stateside, in Denver. I spent a few days there locked up. Officers came and told me that I was in quarantine because I might have been exposed to the disease that had killed all those people."

Linda could hardly believe what she was hearing.

"Go on," she said.

"It's not true," he insisted, "it was no disease that killed these people. I know because I saw the bodies. All of them had been shot, execution style. Years ago, I used to watch documentaries about Nazi concentration camps in Europe and what happened there. Now I find that our side, the ones supposed to be doing what's right, that we are doing the exact same thing. What I saw was genocide. There's no other way to describe it. I made them think that they had convinced me, but I know what I saw! They told me if I said anything publicly, they would come after me and my family. They would deny the event ever happened and lock me up for good."

Sam got up, went over and stared out the window, still continuing to drink his beer.

"It's so strange to be back home," he said as he watched the outside street, "I never thought they'd let me go. Now all of this now seems so... unreal, as if I am just dreaming it."

Linda got up, went over to him and put her arms around him. He turned and embraced her. Then both of them wept.

Mr Balding walked into the police station. He had never really visited many of them outside of the city. This one was small and pokey. There seemed to be just one main room which was separated in half by a reception counter aimed to keep the public away from the office desks. On one side of the room there were doors; Balding reckoned that they were likely to lead to a locker room and the cells. There were only a few desks in the office space and many were filled with stacks of paper. The room was not very clean and Balding noticed layers of dust on the windows and cobwebs in the corners of the room. It was very different to how they allowed things to be up in the city.

What a mess! he thought.

There was one policeman there. He was sitting behind one of the desks making a phone call. Balding tuned in to what he was saying on the phone.

"Alright, I'll send someone around as soon as possible," he said and hung up the phone.

"Hi," said Mr Balding.

The policeman stood up from his desk and came over to the counter.

"I was hoping you could help me," said Balding, "I've come from Chicago. I used to be a cop and I am doing my old commissioner a favour. He asked me to check into a few things for him and the trail has led me here to this town."

"To be honest with you," remarked the officer, raising a hinged section of the countertop and walking out, "we are under such pressure here as a result of the breakout and everything else. I'm the only cop on the premises and now I have to head out too. So I ain't really got the time to sit down with some old man, no offence, to have a chat."

"I totally understand," said Balding, "how about I tag along with you?"

The cop looked at him up and down.

"Alright then."

They headed out the door and got into the police car that was parked out front.

"So, Mr...?"

"Balding."

"What can I do for you?" the cop asked as he pulled away from the kerb.

"I was wondering if anything out of the ordinary has been going on in these parts. You mentioned a breakout?"

"Yeah. They were transporting a prisoner down to the hospital here when the bus crashed and ended up in the river with six people dead and the prisoner either dead or missing."

"So you don't know whether he's dead-meat or out there on the street someplace, or gone into hiding."

The cop nodded.

"My bet is that he drowned with the others."

"We thought that too until yesterday when we pulled the bus out the river and found that the back door had been unlocked."

"Unlocked! Who was the prisoner?"

"Silas, but he was known as 'The Butcher'."

The cop pulled in outside the hospital and they both got out. At the front of the hospital several people were arguing and having a go at each other. The cop just calmly pulled out his notebook and walked over to the chaotic scene. Mr Balding sat back against the door of the car and watched as the officer went to work.

"Alright then! Everybody calm down! Someone tell me what's going on."

"You! What's your name?" the officer asked a woman in the group.

She answered, "Sarah."

"Ok, Sarah, what happened here?"

"I was taking one of our patients from the ward for a stroll around the garden when he suddenly jumped up and ran off into the forest."

The cop rolled his eyes, dismayed at the thought of another escapee. However, he quickly focussed again as the furore continued.

"You let him go," screamed Margie, Sarah's colleague, lashing out.

With that, the fight started up again forcing the officer to separate the parties again.

Then Mr Balding's phone rang. He looked at the caller ID; it was the commissioner. He walked away from the noise and answered him.

"Hello, sir."

"Yeah, where are you now, Balding?"

"I've just arrived here in Hope."

"Good, good! Listen, I want you to visit a man there. He is a pastor of a GIBO International Church. I'll text you his address."

"Ok."

The commissioner hung up and seconds later the text came through. As he walked back towards the crowd he saw that the officer had handcuffed young lady called Sarah and was putting her into the back of the police car.

Mr Balding went over and sat into the front seat.

In the back, she was now crying.

He turned to her and said, "Don't worry. By the looks of it, he's just taking you away to help calm the others down. He'll probably let you go free as soon as we get back to the station."

This helped her. She sniffed and began to calm down a little.

Silas scraped out the last piece of food from the tin.

He realised his situation, *I need to go and find some food*, he said to himself.

He remembered the house that he had raided and considered for a moment the possibility of going back there to steal from them again. But immediately he recalled his ordeal and all the dreams that he had been having lately about his victims. It was heart-wrenching. All his life he had got by without his conscience affecting him on account of things that he did. On one occasion, he had actually shot a man dead despite knowing that he was a father of six children. It had meant nothing to him then. Yet now, it had become everything. Every night since his escape, the dreams kept coming with a greater intensity to the extent that he now even dreaded falling asleep.

A REMNANT HOPE

"What am I to do for food then?" he asked, looking upwards.

There was no response.

"Hhhmph," he said in annoyance, "God, if you are there and if it is you who's been hounding me about my past, then help me not to go back and steal but..."

He stopped.

"Hhhmph," he said again, this time as an expression of his unbelief.

He stood up to look out of the window. Then, just as he looked, he saw, right there on the grass outside, several rabbits. Suddenly memories flashed into his mind about how, when he was a child, his uncle had taught him to catch rabbits by setting traps.

He looked around the hut and found some string that he could use and then watched the rabbits to find the particular paths that they were taking. He made a loud noise and watched as they all ran towards the safety of their burrows, and took a mental note of their routes. He ran outside and quickly began to set traps.

With any luck, he thought, *I'll be having rabbit-stew for breakfast.*

When he had finished, it was beginning to get dark so he gathered some wood for the fire and settled down for the night. His stomach was still rumbling as he closed his eyes. But he found that the hope of food in the morning was enough satisfaction for now.

His dreams began again.

He was in the cabin but he was floating up near the ceiling and looking down at himself. He began to see the scene which had happened earlier in the day when he was sitting on the bed. Not only could he see himself but the walls of the cabin were transparent and he could see outside the cabin as well. It was as if his eyes had developed a kind of x-ray vision. As he floated there, time suddenly began to slow and he heard himself speak.

"God, if you are there..."

Suddenly he saw a bright white light come shining into the room. It was so bright that he had to cover his eyes for a few seconds until his eyes adjusted. When he looked he saw that a man, dressed in white, was now standing next to his bed.

"And if it's you who's been hounding me about my past," Silas heard himself say.

The man in white immediately stepped forwards, passed through the wall and was outside the house. He began to take rabbits as if out of nowhere and place them on to the grass.

Silas heard himself speak again.

"Then help me not to go back steal but..."

The man in white came back into the cabin. Silas now saw himself standing over at the window, seeing the rabbits on the grass. Then the man in white looked up at Silas as he floated there and said, "Ask and you will receive, seek and you will find."

"Who are you?" Silas asked, his voice trembling. But the man had vanished and Silas was left there watching the scene from earlier that day and how he had made the traps for the rabbits.

Can this be how it happened? Did God hear what I said and put those rabbits on the grass for me to catch?

With that, Silas woke from his dream. He sat up, his feet dangling over the edge of the bed. He felt a chill snatching at his ankles. He got up, stoked the fire, and threw on some more logs.

"I'm too tired to think through this now," he remarked.

Then he lay back exhausted on the bed and closed his eyes.

Luke sat patiently. He was in a car parked next to an alley in downtown Houston.

"This is where they are," he said out loud.

After crossing the border he had stolen a mobile phone and had called a number. Just like all the way through his journey, he knew that he was alone and was in receipt of help and knowledge from dark forces. When he dialled the number, he happened to get connected a phone-conference where several important people were discussing matters of national security and talking about tracking down a group of people that they referred to as 'fanatics'. On an impulse, he had spoken up saying that he had accepted the task of finding a little girl. One man of authority, a senator, took notice of what he said and agreed to help him. From that moment, Luke had followed his instructions to the letter and knew that he was to wait where he was.

Twenty minutes went by. It was at the dead of night and he was in the roughest part of town. It was not the kind of place where any decent person would want to hang out but he was here, looking for people to help him in a sinister task. Two men came strolling out of the alley dressed like bikers with leather clothing. One of them had a red bandana on his head. They began to walk away so Luke started the engine and began to follow them. As he got near them he honked his horn and this made them jump. Annoyed by the disturbance, they turned and walked quickly towards him.

"Hey, man, what the hell are you doing?" said one of them, kicking at the door of the car.

Luke cared nothing for the car as it was stolen. He opened his door and got out and the two men came around to his side of the car and stood face to face with him. He could tell from their expressions that they were just about to beat him up and hijack the car.

"Jones," he said, once again receiving knowledge from an unknown source. He suddenly knew about these men, their names and what kind of people they were.

They stopped in their tracks and looked at him, confused.

"And Rob?"

"Who are you, fool? How come you know our names?" they raged, pushing him back against the car.

"Relax, I came here looking for you," said Luke.

"Who sent you? What do you want?"

"You two came highly recommended and I need your help to do a job."

"Oh yeah," said Rob, "we're famous are we?"

"Who's got the big mouth?" Jones asked.

"Does it matter?" Luke said shortly.

Then, realising more fully what Luke had been saying, the men's attitude changed.

"Okay, okay! So what's this job, man?" enquired Rob.

"There is someone who needs to be eliminated."

"Oh yeah?" said Jones, "your wife!" grinning at his own attempt at humour.

"No," said Luke, "actually, it's a girl, a little girl."

"You serious, man?" asked the two together.

"Yes, and any of her 'friends' that get in your way," replied Luke.

"That's heavy, man! I ain't doin' that," said Rob.

"Fifty-grand for doing it," said Luke, almost offhandedly. "Each," he added.

That got their attention and from then on Luke knew that he had them under his control.

Then he sat back into the car.

"Come on, then!" he said, "we have some driving to do."

The two men jumped in, one in the front, the other in the back.

"Where are we headed?" they asked.

A REMNANT HOPE

He shrugged his shoulders. Then he pulled out from the kerb and began to drive. Just then his phone rang.

"Luke, I got your message," the senator said.

"Good! So, where is the girl?"

"She's in a town called Hope."

"Text me the address."

"Ok! And listen, I'll be there too. I will arrive tomorrow."

"There is no need," groaned Luke.

"I have old friends there, people who can help us."

"What kind of help are you talking about?"

"For starters, a place to stay that won't draw suspicion."

"Ok, but you'd best not get in our way. There is no going back for me."

"Nor for any of us."

"Then it's settled. Call me tomorrow when you hit town."

Figures dressed in white darted through the sky. They had wings on their backs and they came to the town of Hope and settled on the houses that they had been sent to. Inside those houses, people began to dream of a place, and how to get there. Many were called but only a few would respond. The same white figures had brought the message to other places further afield but now, the night before the event, they had come to bring the message to the local people telling them that the time has come for them to meet and then go forth because darkness was coming and would try to destroy everything good. But, there is hope like never before, for a way had been made through the darkness, a safe path and, because of it, great things were about to happen.

Michelle let her foot lift from the accelerator when she saw the first sign for the border. She had called ahead and arranged to meet with Fabio, one of the border police. He had agreed to talk to her about what had happened but his shift would finish at midday. She had been driving like a maniac to reach the border in time. She checked her watch; it was already eleven.

Down the road, a mile ahead, she caught her first glimpse of the border gates. As she approached, she made sure to keep within the speed limits to make sure that nobody would open fire on her. Not that they might do that here but, being a reporter, she had heard many bad stories of what border police in other countries do to people at checkpoints.

Thank God this is America! she thought as the memory of those stories flashed through her mind.

At the crossing, there was a queue of traffic. She wound down her window, stuck her head out and saw that she was behind about ten other cars. She waited patiently as each person and car was checked over by the police. Finally, it was her turn and she eased her car forwards.

An officer raised his hand signalling for her to stop and stepped in front of the car. She responded and stopped her car.

"Turn off the engine please, mam and step out of the vehicle."

She obeyed promptly.

"Documents?" said the officer firmly.

She felt as though his gaze was like x-ray vision, that he was even able to analyse her by her expressions and body language.

"They're in my purse."

A REMNANT HOPE

He indicated that she could get them and she leaned in to reach for them. She forgot that she was quite scantily dressed and a wolf-whistle from someone nearby soon reminded her of it. She quickly stood up straight, fixed her skirt and handed the documents to the policeman, feeling rather embarrassed.

He checked through them and compared her face with her photo.

"You're good to go," he announced.

"Thanks," she said.

Then she asked, "Oh by the way, is there an officer called Fabio here?"

"Fabio? Yeah, he's in the office. When you go through the gate, over to the left there is a cark park. You can leave your car there."

"Thanks," she said as she got back into her car.

She started up the engine and drove forwards, the barriers lifted and she went through and drove straight into the car park and found a space. She got out of the car and went straight to the office. The door was locked but she found a bell-push and pressed it. A voice answered her from an intercom speaker fixed to the wall.

"Who is it?"

"It's Michelle from Channel Seven" she answered, "I'm here to see officer Fabio."

The door buzzed and she walked through into a reception area which was nicely decorated. She could tell that this area was not for the general members of the public. Separated from the reception area were a number of other rooms and some of these had signs on the doors – Interview room A, Interview room B, and so on.

A police officer came down the stairs and into the room. He stood about six feet tall and was quite thinly built. He wore square framed glasses.

"Michelle?"

"Hi, yes", she said, "Fabio?"

"That's me, we can talk in here," he said stepping towards one of the side-rooms and beckoning for her to follow. He opened the door and switched on the light. Once inside, he closed the door and they sat down with a table between them.

"So, what can you tell me about what went on here?" she asked.

"I was on duty that day," Fabio explained, "and I was checking incoming vehicles when a man approached the pedestrian gate. I think that I might have even caught a glimpse of him out of the corner of my eye but I'm not sure. Checking cars can be an intense job. As you never know what you might find, it takes a lot of concentration."

"I'm sure," said Michelle, nodding.

"It was about half an hour later when the alarm went off. At the change of shifts, Simon came on duty, and found the two guys who operate the pedestrian gate, dead."

"How had they died? Were they shot?" Michelle enquired.

"No, no, nothing like that. They sit behind bulletproof glass."

"Then what did the medics say when they got here?"

"They said it was heart failure. But, then I saw the tapes and listened to the voices, I knew it was something different."

At this he took some photographs out of an envelope and showed them to her.

"Here is one of a man standing at the pedestrian gate. You can see that he is talking to the two guys in the office."

"Oh," said Michelle, "it's a pity we can't see his face."

"I know. Then here is this one where the guys have dropped to the floor and you can see the guy beyond, stepping through the gates."

"It's blurred," Michelle observed.

"Yes and it is like that on the video too. It gets all blurred but then comes clear again after he is gone."

"Who or what do you reckon could do something like that?"

"I don't know, and to be honest, Michelle, it freaks me out."

"Hmmm!"

"And here, this was the last photo taken of him. It was taken just on the edge of the checkpoint area."

Michelle took one look and sat up straight. It was Luke in the flesh, as clear as day. Her jaw dropped as she gazed at him. Suddenly the memory of the fear which she had seen in the eyes of the people that she had already interviewed came back to her and a shiver ran down her spine.

"What is it?" the policeman asked her.

"Nothing," she lied.

"You recognise him, don't you?" he said.

"Maybe."

"Look," he pleaded, "one of those guys who died was my brother-in-law. If you know something, then please tell me."

"It's a man named Luke Tyrell," said Michelle.

"Luke Tyrell, Luke Tyrell. Why does that name ring a bell?" responded Fabio.

"It's been all over the news for the last few weeks – you know - the missing plane."

"The missing plane!" the officer gasped, examining the photo once again to get a better look at Luke Tyrell.

CHAPTER 8

A DAY OF HOPE

Mr Balding had talked with the police officer after his call to get a bit more information and then he had found himself a room in a guest house for the night, deciding to leave it to the next day before going out to the pastor's house. During the evening he had strolled around town, soaking up the atmosphere and hoping to bump into one or more of those people that he had photos of. But he had no luck.

The next day he followed directions that he had got from the police officer and drove down a lane that led from Hope towards the lake. The officer had told Balding that he had been there several times before for summer barbeques that the pastor and his wife normally held a few days before heading back to Chicago. It was usually a big social event for the town, enough to make most people have respect for the pastor in spite of hardly knowing him at all. The policeman had also told Balding about the pig-on-a-spit that the pastor himself would cook.

On the lane, Balding saw some people who were walking along.

They must be going to the lake too, he thought.

He slowed and passed them with care as the lane was not very wide and he wanted to try and look at their faces too. After passing them, he saw two spectacular big black gates. He had been told that they would be closed but, instead, they were open as if someone was expecting him. So he drove straight up the drive and parked behind the pastor's car outside the front of the house. He got out and looked around. The gardens were green and luscious and the view of the lake was breathtaking.

I can see why someone would want to build a house here, he said to himself.

He walked past the pastor's car and up three stone steps to the front door and rang the bell.

A woman opened the door. She had a very pleasant face and bright eyes, and she stood as tall as he was.

"Hi, I'm Mr Balding," he said.

The woman just stared at him blankly.

"I am looking for the pastor."

Her face brightened. "Oh sure, come on in," she said, opening the door wide for him to enter.

"I'm Gloria, the pastor's wife. I must apologise about the state of the gardens. We are currently looking for a new gardener."

This woman must have high expectations, Mr Balding said to himself. To him, the garden looked great.

"Are you here for the meeting?" Gloria enquired.

"Actually, I was asked to come here to see the pastor. I was told that he could help me."

"Help you with?"

"Things that the police commissioner in Chicago has sent me to look into."

"Ahh, we know the commissioner there! How is he doing?"

"Fine."

She indicated for Balding to follow her.

"You can sit in here," she said, showing him into a room. "This is the library."

Balding looked around. The walls of the room were covered from floor to ceiling with bookshelves. It was quite a collection. In the centre of the room was a large conference-sized table with several chairs placed around it.

"Please take a seat," said Gloria. "Would you like any refreshments? Tea? Coffee?"

"Oh I'd love a coffee, thank you," Balding said graciously as he sat down on one of the chairs that were around the table.

She returned after a couple of minutes with a pot of coffee and two cups. Just as she was pouring, the pastor walked in. Mr Balding stood up to greet him with a handshake.

"Hello! Mr Balding is it? I heard the commissioner sent you. How is old Reggie doing?"

"He is doing quite well."

"He will be doing a lot better when he retires," the pastor said with a grin. Balding didn't want to agree but he gave a quick nod.

The pastor sat down at the head of the table and his wife poured him a cup of black coffee. She then left them to talk, closing the door behind her as she left.

"So, what can I do for you?" asked the pastor.

"I've come to look for any religious fanatics who might be in the area. In fact I'm fairly sure that they could be having a meeting right here in town today."

"Ah, he has sent you to infiltrate them."

"He told you about that?" asked Balding, surprised at his answer.

"Let's just say that it's not the first time that Reggie has sent people to our door. So, you say they are in town and are going to have a meeting today?"

"Yes."

"Are you sure?"

"Yes, I think so. All over their social networks they are talking about an 'HSP' that is going to happen today," he explained.

"And they say that it's to take place here in Hope?"

"Not exactly, but I have a gut feeling that it is."

"Oh, you know what, I think that could be right," said the pastor, "in fact, some other out-of-towners have come here as well looking for these fanatics. It's a strange co-incidence perhaps? They have come on a much more delicate matter than just locating them. We have information that they have abducted at least one child, who we believe to be in danger."

The pastor looked at Balding to gauge his reaction and could see that he believed that it was credible. So, he continued. "A group of us are about to meet here to discuss what we can do to locate these people. Perhaps you would stay and join us. Maybe we can help each other."

Mr Balding quickly accepted his invitation. At least he was getting somewhere.

Mr Smith parked his car, strolled along the street and into the only hardware store in town.

"Good afternoon Mr Smith. Doing some more work

at the house?"

"No, not today," Smith replied, "I'm going to take a break and go for a walk. But, I need a few things to take with me."

"Sure, sure, what do you need?"

Smith reached into his pocket and pulled out a list.

This is so strange, doing this, he thought.

During a dream the night before, he had been told that he needed to come into town and buy these things at the hardware store and then go for a walk down by the lake.

"Okay," said Smith, reading out the items he needed, "I need a torch, the brightest one you have as well as batteries for it and some spares. I also need a map of the local area, a sharp knife, and a canteen, a rucksack if you have one, a sleeping bag and a tent."

"Sounds more like a camping trip than a walk," remarked the shopkeeper.

"I guess so."

The storekeeper began to gather all the requested items and place them on the counter.

Then, remembering things for the house, Smith said, "Oh and I also need some eight by four plasterboard sheets for the house and some plaster."

"What quantity of each?"

"Twelve sheets, and three bags."

"I'll have to order those in."

"That's fine but I'll pay for it all now though."

"Of course. Now as to tents. I don't have many in stock. You could have either a one man tent or a large family tent."

"Hmm. I'll take the one-man."

As the shopkeeper gathered the last few bits and began to check the items through at the till, Smith went to browse around the shop. He saw a large tool set which he considered he might come back and buy because most of the tools at the house were old and worn.

"Okay, that will be 560 dollars for everything," said the storekeeper as Smith returned to the counter.

Mr Smith reached for his wallet and paid him in cash. Then he took the bags from the counter.

"Give me a shout when the plaster can be delivered," he said over his shoulder as he left.

"No problem. Thanks Mr Smith."

As Smith walked out into the afternoon air, he saw something that stopped him in his tracks. Right across the street, parked outside the diner, was senator Holloway's black Mercedes.

"Can't be!" Smith gasped.

Then he saw the senator's driver coming out of the diner carrying two coffees and handing them into the back of the car. Smith ducked down behind the cars parked on his side of the road.

"What's he doing here? How does he know that I am here?" he muttered to himself.

Smith kept down and edged along the pavement towards his own car hoping that they would not spot him. He took a quick look across the street and saw the driver getting into the car.

I need to follow them and find out where they are going, he thought to himself.

At the risk of being seen, he stood up and walked faster. When he got to his own car, he threw the things he'd bought on to the back seat, quickly sat into the driving seat and started the engine. Already the senator's car had pulled out and was driving off towards the lake. Smith pulled out from the kerb and followed.

The senator's car had blackened windows. He could not see in but he was aware that they would be able to see out, and see him. What he did not know was that Lisa was in the car and she had seen him as soon as he had stepped out of the store. She had shown no reaction because she didn't want to alert the senator who was sitting beside her but she had wished that she could have called out to Smith for help.

Shortly after she had last seen Smith, she had confronted the senator about his various affairs and this had led to a huge argument that had turned violent. The result was a trip to hospital with her body covered in bruises. The senator had attacked her in such a vicious way that night that she had thought that she was going to die.

Now the senator was having her accompanied everywhere, either by himself or by one of his cronies. There seemed to be no escape from such a powerful man. But, at the sight of Smith, her heart felt a glimmer of hope. She knew that he had loved her deeply and that she had walked away from that and now she longed for him again. Maybe it was because of what had happened between her and her husband, or perhaps it was something even deeper inside her heart.

As soon as Val turned the key in the door and opened it, Harold immediately confronted him.

"Where on earth have you been?" he demanded, hardly allowing Val to step inside the door.

"I'm sorry, I didn't mean to take so long," Val said apologetically.

"Here, I brought some food," he said, handing Suzie a bag of takeaway Chinese food.

"Thanks," she said as she eyed Harold in an attempt to calm him down. Then turning her head, she called out, "Come Jenny, it's time for dinner."

Since fleeing their house the night before, they had been hiding out in a motel just outside of Hope. Val had left early in the morning without any indication of where he had gone and Harold had got more and more irate about the situation as the day had gone on.

"Come on, Jenny," Suzie repeated.

Jenny looked, turning away from the TV.

"Oh, hi, uncle," she said.

She came over and hopped up on to the bed where Suzie was removing the boxes of food from the bag.

"Is everything okay?" Harold whispered as he leaned closer to Val.

"I had to take care at every step to make sure I wasn't being followed," Val replied quietly.

"In case the bad men follow you," Jenny blurted loudly just before biting down on her first mouthful of food.

"That's right Jenny," confirmed Val, now speaking louder.

Harold began to calm down and sat on the edge of the bed, pausing for a moment before taking some of the food that was laid out.

"Any problems at this end?" asked Val, taking off his sweater.

"Do you mean besides being locked up here all day?" said Harold, still not fully calm yet.

"Harold, stop it," said Suzie. "No, Val, sorry. There were no problems and no-one called."

"Good," sighed Val, finding a chair. He took some food and began to eat.

"It's going to be a tough journey tonight, so eat as much as you can," he said. "I had to pick up everything for the meeting tonight and, as we can never tell how many are coming; it's always a bit of a challenge. More people get invited than what show up," he admitted, "but that's the root of the problem. Everyone has heard God's call at some point in their lives but not everyone has responded. Some haven't even realised that God was speaking to them."

"And where is the meeting tonight?" asked Harold.

"In the forest, down near the lake," answered Jenny, her face beaming.

Harold looked at Jenny, not understanding how she knew and he didn't.

"Listen Harold," said Val, "the normal way for someone to get to the meeting is that they will already know how to find it. You and Suzie are the only exceptions that we've ever had. We don't normally bring people along who have not had the dreams or visions about the meeting."

"Why not?"

"It protects us from spies."

"Oh."

"It doesn't matter and I'm sure the others will understand. You just have to come. Decisions have to be made at the meeting about what we're going to do about Jenny."

"We know," agreed Harold, nodding.

"How's your food, Jenny?" asked Suzie, trying to take some of the tension out of the atmosphere.

"I like this one the best," Jenny pointed out, "it makes my mouth tingle."

"It's called Hot n' Spicy Beef," Suzie explained.

Val continued eating without further conversation. He was deep in thought. He had no idea who would be at the meeting that night or what the outcome might be. One thing was clear, though. The family seated on the bed in front of him were going to have a lot more upheaval ahead of them.

When they had all finished eating, they packed up all their belongings and loaded them into the truck that Val had come in, and waited while Val went and paid at reception for the use of the room. Val had got a different vehicle during the day, one of the several steps he had taken to throw anyone who could be following them off the scent. He had rented a truck using the name 'Mr Roberts' and had paid in advance for three month's rental. All this came to five-fifty dollars, the exact amount that had been given to him by Linda. He knew that the truck would probably be taken by Harold at the end of the night. It was one of those big four by fours. It was less than a year old and was equipped with extras such as a SatNav and heated seats.

They all climbed into the truck and Val drove them towards town. Before they got there, Val took a right turn down a dusty lane that led into the depths of the forest. He immediately pulled off that lane and drove in between two trees and halted and waited there for twenty minutes to make sure that they were not being followed. Content that they were alone, he reversed back on to the lane and continued to drive deeper into the forest.

"This is an old hunting track," he explained, "they'd drive this way to the hunting lodges near the lake but most of those are deserted nowadays."

He pointed out of the window as they passed by an old building which was in a dilapidated state with its roof caved in. The truck was bouncing up and down on account of the uneven condition of the track and the further they went, the worse it got.

"I didn't know that all this was here," said Harold, looking around.

"Nor do most of the townspeople," replied Val, "it's probably a good thing, considering."

"Then, how do you know where to go?"

"I saw it in a dream," said Val, then speaking over his shoulder, he asked, "Jenny, in your dream, how did you get to the meeting?"

"In your truck, uncle," she said, quite calm about the whole thing.

"See, the dreams are prophetic," said Val, "they show you how something will happen and they can be very detailed."

"I still can't my head around it," exclaimed Suzie.

"Good! Neither can the police!" joked Val.

After a mile or two, Val turned right again. This time they went off the track and even deeper into the forest. It was quite a job navigating through it but, after ten minutes of jostling over rough terrain, they came across a path of sorts, followed it and came to a cabin that was surrounded by trees.

"This is it. Now, Jenny, all of you. Whatever you do, do not go inside that cabin."

"Why not?" asked Suzie.

"It's highly dangerous, that's all. Well, that's what I heard in my dream," explained Val.

He stopped the truck halfway between the trees and the back of the cabin. Then he took Harold with him, leaving the other two in the truck. The two men began to collect wood for a fire; darkness was coming and they needed light.

Sarah paced the floor of her cell.

Now I know what it felt like for John to be locked up. He told me that everything would be okay and yet here I am locked up in jail and probably fired from my job. Dear God, she prayed, *I know that I have to reach that bonfire tonight. Please help me get out of here. I don't care what happens with my job but I do need to see Steve. I need to understand what's going* on.

The door opened and there stood the same police officer who brought her in.

"Sarah, you can go now," he said.

"At last!" she said, pushing past him and almost knocking him to one side.

"Easy now," the officer said. "You can change back into your clothes in there," he said pointing to a locker room and handing her back her belongings. She immediately picked up her phone and looked at the screen.

Seven missed calls from Steve! He must have been worried about me! She scrolled down to his name to call him back but the battery died and the phone switched itself off.

"Damn it!" she said aloud.

She quickly changed and went back out to the policeman who was waiting to see her off the premises.

"The hospital has let the matter go," he said.

"What about my job?" she asked.

The policeman shrugged his shoulders.

"You'll have to contact them about that yourself," he said.

"I didn't even do anything," she insisted, proclaiming her innocence once again.

"Lady, we found a witness who saw you speaking to the man and, when he got up and ran off, you didn't even try to follow him."

"Would you follow a man who was considered dangerous, all by yourself into the woods, without anyone knowing where you were? Oh, maybe you would, but I'm a girl. There's no telling what he might have done to me," retorted Sarah, defending herself.

"Look, just drop it. They obviously have."

"Did they find the man yet?"

"Who?"

"The patient. John."

"No! The judge wouldn't give us a search-warrant for your house," the policeman said sarcastically, "don't you worry, he'll probably turn up somewhere, a vagrant like that. It's probably best to just let him go his own way, maybe on to the next town. I say good riddance to him."

The policeman escorted her out of the building. She was on foot, her car being still up at the hospital. So she decided to go there first and find out what was the situation was regarding her job.

At the hospital, she was asked to wait at reception. The head nurse soon came down from the wards to see her.

"Look, Sarah," she said sternly, "I don't know what went on yesterday but we have to look into the matter. So, I am afraid that I will have to suspend you until we get to the bottom of this."

"But I didn't do anything! He just ran and I couldn't follow him," complained Sarah.

The head-nurse's attitude softened a little.

"Don't get upset, Sarah," she said, reaching out and touching Sarah's forearm, "just leave the whole thing to due process. It will all work out, you'll see."

"Okay," said Sarah, "will you call me and let me know what develops?"

"Of course! Look, I have to go now, you know how it is here, all go."

"Yes... okay... thanks! See you."

"Bye, Sarah," called the head nurse, already headed back in the direction of the wards.

Sarah left the building and walked into the garden.

That doesn't sound too bad, she thought, *I guess I could always sue them for having me locked up if they don't allow me to come back.*

She noticed that it was starting to get dark.

I wonder if I follow the directions that I got in my dream, will I find Steve somewhere out there in the forest? she asked herself as she looked at the forest that came right up to the end of the garden.

Sam held the bottle of ketchup in his hand, finding all that he was hearing totally incredible.

"So you're telling me that our George, somehow, made more ketchup appear in this bottle."

"That's it exactly," answered Linda.

He laughed with scorn in his voice.

"And also, when they met the little girl, each of them was healed right there in the middle of the store! Within seconds, they went from puking to scoffing down chocolate," she reminded him.

"Maybe they just recovered," he said, still searching his mind for a rational answer.

"I'm not crazy!" retorted Linda.

"That's not what I'm saying. I'm just wondering if there might be another explanation."

"Such as?"

"I don't know. It's hard for me to get my head around this, you know."

"I think God did it," said Linda, finding the courage to blurt out her answer.

"Look baby, don't get me wrong. I'm glad to hear that you are in touch with God. For years I've been looking forward to us being able to say grace together and so on but…"

"Well if it's not God, then what is it?" answered Linda, challenging him.

Sam spoke slowly. "I went to church for years when I was a child. Then, when the old system was outlawed and the International Church came in, I attended there for years as well but I've never heard of anything like this before – dreams, miracles and people getting healed. If it is God who is doing these things, then why didn't I see them happen at church?"

"I don't know," said Linda, "maybe there's something wrong with the church."

"Don't say that, that's blasphemy!" snapped Sam.

"No, it is not!"

"Yes it is," persisted Sam.

"That kind of thinking is what made it possible for priests to abuse people for years," she said promptly.

"That was years ago," he countered. "They thoroughly vet pastors and priests today using psychological tests and everything."

"You just don't understand," said Linda.

"I do. I just find it hard to believe that's all, and especially now when you're saying that you have to go out tonight and bring the children. You want to take them to some place in the middle of nowhere in order to meet with other people who will also find the place from what they saw in their dreams. It's just plain crazy!"

"I thought you said that I wasn't crazy," said Linda, still standing up for herself.

"I didn't say 'you' I said 'it's just crazy'."

"Well I'm definitely going..." she announced.

Sam shook his head at her.

"You must have blown a fuse," he said derisively.

"I'm going to go Sam," she said louder this time.

He looked at her scornfully. "Fine! Go to your silly made up nonsense but don't bother calling me if you get lost out there in the dark."

He took out his phone and removed the battery out of the back of it. "There! Good luck to you if you get lost," he snapped at her.

"That's real nasty, Sam," she sniffed, tears forming in her eyes, "is that how I treated you when you came home in a state? No, I loved you and listened to you and tried to understand all that you told me. All I ever asked you for is for some support to help me and the children. They saw tonight's meeting in their dreams too. Can you explain that? If you can't believe me, then at least believe them."

He turned his back on her in a temper and stood looking out of the window.

She turned around, took the car keys and quickly jumped into the car where the children were already waiting, safely belted into their seats. As she reversed off the drive, Sam came running out.

"There's no dirt track just outside of town anyway! Good luck finding it!" he bellowed after them.

Michelle pulled in at the first gas station that she could find on the road that came from the border checkpoint. She decided to fill up with gas there rather than trust her car to make it all the way.

I might be driving all day, she reckoned.

She got out of the car and went into the store and up to the counter. A young man stood there behind the till.

"Gas on number one, fifty dollars worth," she said, handing him fifty dollars in cash. Then she looked hopefully at him and asked, "Have you got a fax machine here that I could use?"

"Yea, lady, it's over there. It costs one dollar per sheet."

"A dollar? Really! Here's five."

She ran out to her car and grabbed her copy of the photos. Returning, she went over to the fax machine and entered the appropriate digits for the editor's fax machine.

Wait till he sees these. He is going to get some buzz out of it, she thought to herself in a buoyant mood.

As soon as the three photos had been copied and transmitted, she dialled his number from her cell-phone. It rang for ages before he picked up.

"What do you want?" he asked abruptly.

"That's no way to treat your best reporter," she answered coyly.

He laughed.

"Got a story then?" he asked sarcastically.

"I sure do, boss."

"You're kidding!"

"Nope. Are you near your fax machine?"

"No. Hang one sec."

Michelle heard him open the door of his office.

"Okay," he said, "what am I looking at here?"

"You are looking at what will become the most famous photos of the year. There are two photos of Luke Tyrell talking to border police and then one of him crossing the border into the U.S."

"Holy crap!" said the editor, delighted.

"Also," continued Michelle, "those two police you see in the photo…"

"Yeah?"

"They're dead."

"How?"

"Nobody knows. They were alive when they began to talk to Luke but were dead when he had finished with them. Then, the border gate just opened all by itself as if by magic."

"So, Luke is alive and on some sort of rampage?"

"It seems like it. Some of those who found him on the beach are dead too. I found one witness though, an old man who was there when Luke was found. I have their statements here as well."

"Okay, this is almost too good to be true. I'm going to run it in tomorrows' news."

"What line are you going to go with?" she asked excitedly.

"'Luke found alive in Mexico' maybe but I'm not sure yet. By the way, we need you back here. Whereabouts are you at the moment?"

"I'm about an hour north of Houston at a gas station in the middle of nowhere. I'm driving the whole way back as there weren't any flights out of Houston until tomorrow."

"Okay, do that. We may have to interview you over the phone if you can't make it back in time, so make sure you keep your phone charged and also, make sure you have coverage."

"The coverage should be okay."

"This is big, Michelle. I know I doubted you at first but, holy cow, I never expected this."

"Right, I'll talk to you soon. I want to get back on the road."

"Awesome. Bye."

She picked some food off the shelves and went back to the counter.

"I'll take these too," she said, handing the items to the man at the till, "it looks like I'm in for a long drive."

Silas returned from setting the traps for another night of catching rabbits. The previous night had been a huge success and he had caught three and he had eaten each of them in succession for his breakfast, lunch and dinner.

It's time to light the fire and settle down for the night, he thought to himself as he stepped inside the hut.

Just as he shut the door to the lodge he heard a noise that he immediately recognised as that of a car.

"It can't be! Not here," he said out loud in a panicked tone.

Then, as he peered out, he saw lights shining through the trees and could clearly hear the noise of an engine. He reacted instinctively and jumped behind the door pulling his knife out of his pocket.

"I'm not going back to prison," he said to himself in a whisper.

He heard the engine stop and then the sound of two car doors banging shut so he moved over to peer out through the windows again. He could not see the vehicle anywhere. Then, through a side window he saw two men walking along by the line of trees.

If I go now, I might be able to sneak out of here without trouble.

He quickly gathered his belongings and exited by the front door, quietly. There were enough shadows to keep him hidden and he was grateful for them. He hopped down off the porch and ran to the trees opposite where he saw the men. From there he circled around to try and see what they were up to. When he got closer, he saw that the vehicle he'd heard was a truck and that a woman was still sitting in it while the two men were gathering wood and piling it on the ground.

They're making a fire. Why are they making a fire? he wondered.

He waited for a while and watched, making sure to stay low and hidden.

Just after the two men had lit the fire, another man came out from the trees, just next to where Silas was hidden, and walked towards the fire. Silas quickly realised that more people were coming. Alarmed, he fled. He ran for the first two miles and then came to a hedge and jumped over it. He looked around him. He seemed to have entered the grounds of some residence or other as there was a huge mansion there facing the lake. By now, the last bit of sunlight was fading fast.

I'll stay here while I catch my breath, he thought to himself as he chose a spot to hide behind some bushes. He lay there on his side to allow his body to relax, and then he got up to check that no one was approaching his position.

Suddenly, he saw a figure moving through the darkness and sneaking up to the house just like he would have done if he was going to break in. He watched as the person headed directly for a window that was wide open with a light on inside.

"I wouldn't go in that way mate," he muttered to himself.

But, when the man reached the window, instead of climbing in he just sat there, huddled right underneath it.

What are you up to?

When a slight breeze came across the lake and blew past the house, Silas could hear the sound of voices coming from inside the window.

Now I really am curious.

It didn't take him long to decide what to do next. He crawled along the dry grass straight towards the window. About ten feet away from it there was another hedge so he hid behind that. He could just about catch the conversation now. Apparently, it seemed as if some people had just arrived, Silas concluded as he listened closely.

"Ah Luke," Silas heard one of them say, "last but not least! We were wondering when you might show up. This is Senator Holloway and this is his wife Lisa. That's Balding. He's an ex-cop. And that's our local police enforcement representative over there, Officer Mendes. Please do sit down."

There are cops here! Maybe I should get the hell out of here while I can! Silas thought as he listened intently, trying to work out what was happening but especially what the police were up to. He wanted to know if they were looking for him or not.

"Thanks. I brought these two guys with me from Houston, Jones and Rob. Listen! All of you had better understand that the three of us are here just to get the job over and done with. We don't want to mess about or to delay things..." Silas heard Luke say.

Then a voice said, "Noted! Now please take a seat. You are all welcome. Let's get properly started. As most of you know, we are on the trail of fanatics whom we all believe to be meeting somewhere in this area. Mr Balding here has informed us that they may be even having a meeting tonight, somewhere near here, perhaps in the forest..."

I wonder if that was them who were lighting the fire, Silas surmised.

"...or in someone's house," the speaker continued, "in the past it has been notoriously hard to get intelligence on these meetings. Our most pressing reason for coming is that we suspect them of abducting at least one person, a little girl named Jenny Stevens. She was born in Connecticut but several weeks ago her parents were murdered and she went missing. We believe that a local couple in this town seem to have been established as substitute parents, using falsified documents to claim that they adopted her. Officer Mendes went the check their place today but they have already fled. Perhaps they got wind that we were on the way. We don't know where they are right now but most likely, we reckon, they will bring the girl along to the meeting..."

Could she be the girl in my dreams, the one I was trying to protect? Silas wondered.

"So, has anyone any ideas where they might be hiding? Mr Balding, what do you think?"

"I think that they will be meeting in the forest," he replied.

"Why is that?"

"It just makes sense to me. People can gather in a place like that without arousing suspicion. As you know, in this town people can just walk out into their backyards and enter the forest. So it would be very easy therefore to gather a large number of people together. Previously, the only CCTV camera to catch some of their faces was in the hospital garden and it showed people that were heading out into the forest."

"I can see why the commissioner chose you," remarked the speaker. "The problem is that the forest here is huge and practically circles the whole lake. These people would be extremely difficult to find by the few of us gathered here."

"I reckon that if we all split up and head in different directions keeping our phones on, we might just get lucky. We might spot someone walking through the forest, or even see a fire with people gathered around it."

"Luck? You'd want to pin all our hopes on luck?" said one voice.

"These fanatics are probably armed, we need fire-power," said another voice.

"Good point. Officer, did you bring the guns as I requested?"

Silas heard a thump as a heavy bag hit the top of a wooden table. At the sound of that noise, the man who had stayed still under the open window moved again. He headed for the edge of the gardens and hopped over a wall. Silas gave him a head-start and then followed, first looking over the wall and then jumping it.

Lisa jumped with the fright. A red light in the room had suddenly started flashing and a siren had sounded.

"What's that for?" shouted Luke.

"The alarm system has been triggered," said the pastor, opening the door and running out.

They all got up and followed him to a small room at the centre of the house. There was only space for three or four people in the room, so the rest had to peer in over others to see. Lisa couldn't get a look in at all.

The pastor was explaining things as he checked his equipment.

"We have motion sensors and cameras all over this place. It seems like a sensor noticed someone jumping over the wall to the west of the house. I'll rewind the video recording and see," he said as he toggled the controls.

He paused at a point where he saw a man hop the wall. Then he zoomed in on his face.

"It can't be!" gasped the senator.

"You know him?" asked the pastor, looking at the senator in amazement.

"Yes, he works for me, or at least he used to. His name is Smith."

Smith was here. Then maybe he knows that I am here too and he came for me, thought Lisa, hearing what the men were saying.

"But who is that behind Smith?" asked the pastor, pointing at an orange blur on the screen.

"What are you talking about?" said the others in unison, leaning forward to see more clearly.

"See," said the pastor, "there's another person behind Smith. Whoever it is, is dressed in an orange jumpsuit."

He forwarded the video playback, and then zoomed in on the face.

Now it was officer Mendes turn to speak out in shock. "But he's supposed to be dead..." he announced.

"You know him?" said the pastor, "who is he, then?"

"That's Silas, Silas the butcher, the murderer who was in the prison van that crashed at the top of the valley. He must have escaped after all."

Now they all stood in shock, staring at the face on the screen.

"It doesn't look like they know each other," suggested Luke, "maybe Silas is going to kill Smith."

Lisa turned and walked away.

They're all distracted now. It's time for me to make a run for it.

She went back into the library.

I've got to save him, she thought, grabbing a gun from the bag.

She climbed out of the open window, ran towards the garden wall, scrambled over it and ran into the forest.

However, back inside, her escape had been recorded by the security cameras.

"Damn it!" the senator yelled, "Lisa's gone after Smith."

"What do you mean?" demanded the pastor. "What has she got to do with him?"

"That man Smith was her 'bit on the side'. I thought I had dealt with it."

"That explains the bruises," sneered Luke.

At the sound of his comment, the senator threw him a nasty look but Luke paid it no attention.

"The question is, guys, what are we going to do now?" said the pastor.

Officer Mendes was the first to answer, "I have to head back to town and call out the National Guard to hunt for Silas," he said.

"What about our mission? That's what we're here for, remember."

"The National Guard might help with that. I'll tell them there might be fanatics in the area and that they are assisting Silas," answered Mendes.

"Good idea," said the senator.

"I'm going after them," said Balding, eager to get out into the forest and searching.

"I'll come with you," said Luke grinning. Jones and Rob turned and followed them to the library to get guns from the bag of firearms.

"Not loading up?" Luke asked Balding as he grabbed a pistol and loaded it with bullets.

Balding shook his head. He had taken stock of the three men that he had just met and didn't look like child-rescuers to him. In fact, they looked more like child-killers.

"Let's go," said Balding, impatient to get moving.

REVIVAL WELL

CHAPTER 9

HOPE OVERCOMES

Steve stepped out from among the trees and walked towards the bonfire. At the same time, several other people were also arriving, some by foot and others by vehicles, but all of them from different directions. He recognised some of them immediately but not others. Nevertheless he greeted each one with a hug and a smile. Steve noticed that Johnson was already there and was standing next to Val near to the fire and the two of them were directing people as they arrived in what they could do to help out. Steve had been looking forward to congratulating Barbara about her engagement to Johnson but, looking around, noticed that she had not got there yet.

The bonfire had been lit but was still being built up so a few of the men went to collect more wood. Steve went along with them to help but as he walked back to the fire with the second load that he had collected, he saw a face that totally took him by surprise. It was Sarah's. As soon as she saw him, she ran to him, jumped up into his arms and kissed him.

"Oh, I'm so glad you are here!" she said. "Just like in my dream."

"You had one too?" he said, astounded.

She nodded happily.

"Then you believe?"

"I'm starting to, but I don't know where to go from here."

He hugged her again.

"Don't worry about that," he said, "we get guidance from above as we go along."

He released her from the hug and looked her in the eyes.

"Sarah, I am so happy you are here," he said.

"Really? It's just that you seemed so troubled the last time we talked. It seemed as if you didn't want us to continue."

He nodded, and then explained, "This way of life, Sarah, is different. The things that we did, as great as they appeared, were done outside of marriage. That's not godly living and it has all sorts of consequences."

"So, what are you saying, Steve?" she asked, "that it's over between us?"

Tears filled his eyes, and he got down on one knee.

"No Sarah," he said tenderly, "I'm asking you a question. Will you marry me?"

Her response was immediate. She literally jumped into his arms again, hugging him and kissing him until they fell laughing onto the grass.

"I guess that's a 'yes' then," said a deep voice, as another man stepped out from the forest.

"John!" exclaimed Sarah. She got up and greeted him with a hug, leaving her new fiancée to get himself up off the ground.

"Thank you so much, John. You were right, everything has worked out."

"Not quite everything yet. But yes, for you yes."

Then Val and Johnson came over to welcome John.

"It is a great honour to have you with us, John," said Val, "I wasn't sure, but I did hope…"

"Do not worry, brother, I was simply temporarily delayed."

"What could possibly hold you back?" asked Eddie.

"Actually, it was my fault," said Sarah, joining the conversation. "It took me a while to help him get away from the hospital!"

Steve's jaw dropped, "You did that? Wow! I'm amazed," he said.

Then John spoke. His voice was soft but stern.

"I'm just thankful for my Father who guided us all here tonight. Let's all seek him now and pray that the enemy will be overcome in this place and that hope will be restored to the entire earth."

John's voice carried to the ears of all the people who had gathered, now numbering about twenty in all. Sarah listened, weighing up the quality of his words. They were spoken with authority. As she thought about John, her admiration for him grew.

So much respect is being given to John in this place when society classified him as crazy, a hearer of voices, a lunatic and a 'John Doe', she thought.

"As for you two," John said, turning back to the happy couple, "there will be time for marriage later." Then to encourage them, he said, "But for now, focus on prayer and seeking Jesus."

In response, Steve led his fiancée in prayer so that she could learn how to pray. They both got down on their knees and began to pray out loud together.

"Dear Lord," he said, "thank you for this night. We thank you for what you have done and we ask that you would make a way for all our enemies to be overcome. We ask that by your power, hope will survive…"

Silas hopped over the wall. He looked around but could not see the man whom he was following. He feared the worse, but then, ahead of him, he caught sight of a light shining.

He must have a torch, Silas realised.

Silas walked towards the light and found that it was the man that he was looking for. He was picking his steps carefully as he walked through the forest, taking time to stop and look around him. Silas took care to not make a sound especially not to step on a twig and break it.

Thank God, he thought, *I had all that practice the last few days chasing rabbits.*

As the man walked on, he seemed to pause less. He seemed surer of where he was going. Silas concluded that the man must have been trying to find a particular track through the forest. As they continued Silas began to realise that, with his change of direction, the man was headed for where his cabin was and where the bonfire gathering was taking place.

I wonder what is going on there? he said to himself.

Then, from behind him, Silas heard twigs breaking underfoot. Someone was coming. He ducked down immediately and just as well. The man up ahead had also heard the noise and swung around to see if anyone was there. He waited for a moment and then walked on but Silas stayed put. Near to where Silas had stopped was a clump of ferns so he crawled into them and hid, hardly daring to breathe.

I want to see who is following us.

After lying there quietly for a few moments he could clearly hear the sound of someone approaching.

Whoever it is must be following the light of the torch too. That man is a fool.

As the person walked past him, Silas looked up to see who it might be.

A REMNANT HOPE

He was shocked to see that it was a girl in her twenties. Even in the semi-darkness he could see that she was quite good looking and was wearing high heels.

That's hardly the right footwear for walking through the forest, Silas chuckled to himself.

She walked on past, paying no attention to the ferns and unaware of the man hiding in them. Silas reflected on how in days gone by he might have attacked a girl like her but he shook off those dark thoughts and began to consider what he might do next. Before he could make a move, four men appeared suddenly, following along the track where the girl had just walked. They were taking great care not to make a sound but nevertheless they walked along at a steady pace. Silas saw that they had guns in their hands and realised that they must have come from the mansion, from the room where he had heard the people in conversation.

After the men had passed by, he got up carefully and followed. He removed his knife from his pocket and stepped forward stealthily, aware that his life depended on it.

If they hear me, they will shoot to kill.

He began to think over everything that had been happening to him. First there was the girl in the dream who told him about freedom, and then his breaking free from the bus and staying alive. Then he thought about his being haunted by the wrongs he had committed in his life and finally about being brought into obedience. He had learnt that he didn't need to steal to survive.

Now, he thought back to the arrival of the truck at his cabin, *could it be that there was a girl in that truck with the woman I saw? Could the little girl really be there, the one that these guys are looking for?*

He thought again about his first dream, where he had seen the girl on a swing, without parents and left defenceless. He remembered the strong sense of urgency to protect her and how he had felt a tingling sensation run through his body. It was as if he had heard a voice speaking inside his head, 'You *must do all you can to protect this child.*'

Smith saw the bonfire ahead through the trees and knew at once that he had reached the place where he was meant to be. In his dream, he had reached the place while there was still some light.

I lost time back at the house, but I have to warn everybody and, if that girl is here, they have to get her out of here.

He switched off his torch and walked towards the bonfire at a quickened pace and stepped out from the trees into the clearing. There were several trucks there now and possibly as many as forty people gathered together with still more arriving. Smith observed how some of them were on their knees while others were lying on the ground. Some seemed to be praying while others were crying, laughing or singing. The scene caught him completely off guard. He had never seen anything like this before and he didn't recognise even one person in the group.

What do I do now? he wondered.

"Hey, everyone!" he shouted out, not knowing if that was the correct procedure.

Immediately, some of the people turned to look at him. Two men then approached him. One of them looked like he might be homeless the other was well dressed with a green jacket on.

"What is your name?" they asked.

"Smith," he said and nodded at the greeting, "and you are?"

"I'm Johnson, and this is my dear friend John," said the man in the light green jacket, "I haven't seen you here before. By any chance are you related to old Mrs Smith who passed away a few years back?"

"Yes," replied Smith. It dawned on him that this was the man that her mum had written about in her letter.

"I thought so, you look very like her."

"She was my mother. You knew her, didn't you?"

"Yes, she was a very kind lady and she always spoke fondly of you, and always prayed for you too. And now, here you are!"

"Yes, here I am," said Smith, "I want to find out who is in charge here to speak with them urgently."

John smiled at him, "You can talk to me."

Smith looked the man up and down and could scarcely believe that this seemingly homeless man was the 'leader', so he began to look over his shoulder to see who else was about. Then, he noticed Johnson's expression and saw that he was in agreement with what the guy had told him.

"Right, whatever," said Smith a little taken aback, "listen, there's trouble coming. Do you have a little girl here? There's some men back there at a nearby mansion and they are coming to look for her. I'm not sure how many of them will come. They have guns and I have no idea what they plan to do. So, do you have a little girl here? She has to leave right now," said Smith with insistence.

"Calm your heart, Mr Smith, everything will..."

John was interrupted as a young woman came running out of the forest still in her high heels. She pushed John out of the way and threw her arms around Smith.

"Lisa! What are you doing here?" he asked, as she began to cry. In the light of the fire he could see her bruises. "What happened to your face?" he asked her.

"He did it, the senator!" she sobbed.

"You poor thing! Look, you're here with me now and I'll make sure that you're alright," Smith said as he kissed her on her cheek.

"No!" she said, pulling back from him. "They saw you and some other man on the security cameras. They are coming to get you."

Smith saw the desperation in her eyes and began to look around for anyone approaching but he couldn't see anyone for now. He turned to the people and addressed the whole group this time with a loud voice.

"John, listen. Everybody, listen. You need to get out of here. Some men with guns have followed us and it's only a matter of time till they get here," he announced.

"It's okay, I have this," said Lisa, pulling out the gun that she had brought from the mansion.

"Where did you get that?" asked Smith.

"From the big house..."

However, when John saw the gun in her hand, he grabbed it from her and flung it away into the woods.

"Why did you do that?" she demanded angrily. "That was for our protection!"

"My dear," he said, "those who live by the sword, die by the sword. We don't need guns. God is our protector."

He ignored her frown and swung around to walk back towards the fire.

"Gather around, everyone," he called.

Everyone stopped what they were doing and gathered to hear him speak. Some stood, others sat.

"The time has come for you all to hear this message. It has been on my heart for a long time and I want to humbly share it with you."

Then he bowed his head and prayed, "Lord God, my Father, let your word go forth and let nothing interrupt it. In Jesus name, amen."

Smith, holding Lisa by the hand, came over to listen as well. More than anything, he wanted to find out what all the fuss was about.

John finished praying and began to speak to the people gathered: he spoke using parables in the manner of prophets and teachers of old.

"In my vision, I looked and I saw wonders in the heavens. It was as if a huge fire had set the sky aflame. Then, on the earth, I saw a single seed lying there on the ground, and inside that seed was carried hope. No-one knew where the seed had come from for it was God who had placed it there. Nearby, other plants saw the seed lying there on the ground and they wondered, *'What is this seed? We never any saw any seed like this one before'.*"

There was total silence now amongst the crowd. Even the children were listening intently.

"A great wonder lay before them and they did not know what to do with it. However, as they watched, weeds came and tried to snatch away the seed but then, all of a sudden, out of the sky, fire came down and burnt up all the weeds. After that, the other plants were truly amazed at this seed and they began to make plans among themselves to take this seed and sow it and let grow to become a strong plant. Then they would have that strong plant as their king to protect them so that no one could ever succeed in a challenge against them ever again."

John paused allowing the words to soak into the ears of those gathered around him.

"But then the seed spoke to them and said this: *Before my creation, all hope was gone. It had been squeezed from the world just like a sponge emptied of its water. But the Creator has made me, not that I may be your king and rule over you, but to remind you about the hope that comes from believing in Jesus, so that you too may seek to produce seed which will carry hope onwards to other plants. That is why I have come here to you. It is so that you too can procreate as the Creator has called us all to do'."* John paused and coughed, his throat dry.

A young boy stood up and handed John a bottle of water.

"Thanks," said John with a smile.

Then he went on, "So all the nearby plants considered the words that the seed had spoken. Each one asked himself *'is it I that must change? Am I the one who will carry the hope that can change the world?'* From then on, they no longer saw the seed as being a mystery but as an illustration of something that the Creator wanted all of them to produce. This made them glad and they submitted themselves to the will of their Creator. Soon many new seeds were being sown, producing plants that were free from the limits set by the world and free from the schemes plotted by the weeds. They grew to be over-comers, truth-speakers and as lovers of truth they were also lovers of the Creator, God Almighty. That is the vision that the Lord God gave me," said John.

At that very moment, Val stepped forward; holding Jenny by the hand. John nodded at him and he began to speak again.

"This is the seed that I spoke about. Her name is Jenny. She is the child of a couple whose marriage was hidden from the world. She is born free, without a birth certificate or any identity as regards the world's view of things. This is how we must all be from now on, aloof from the world. We must marry before God but not according to the laws of the land. We must have children and trust God to deliver them safely into this world. We must not register their births or allow them to have driving license or a passport. God wants us to keep them free so that the world will be powerless to destroy them."

With that, there was a loud bang. It sounded like thunder and shattered the silence. Everyone froze with fear as Val grabbed at his chest and fell to the ground, blood pouring from a ghastly wound.

Mr Balding couldn't believe what he was seeing. He had had no choice but to stay with the gang and so he followed as Luke strode out into the middle of the people who were gathered, his gun still smoking from the shot he had fired. Now he aimed the gun directly at Jenny. Balding looked around into the faces of those who had gathered and immediately recognised at least three of them from the files the commissioner had given to him.

"I guess that man didn't have to wait to be set free," Luke joked. Then he shouted, "Everyone sit down, I don't want to have to shoot any heroes."

Balding approached Luke cautiously.

"Luke, take it easy," he said, "She's just a little girl. Let's hold out for reinforcements to arrive and then all these people can be locked up for good."

His plea fell on deaf ears. Luke pushed him away with one arm, wanting to address the crowd. Balding quickly took out his stealth phone and pressed the emergency button which would scramble police to come to his location.

"Hopefully they will get here in time," he muttered to himself.

There was a stunned silence as Luke made his intentions clear.

"I haven't come here to capture you or take you to the police. I've just come here to kill this girl," he declared.

With that, shouts of defiance came from the crowd. Suzie tried to protect Jenny but Luke kicked her away and grabbed Jenny roughly in a tight hold.

At that Balding had seen enough and stepped towards Luke to overpower him but Jones grabbed him from behind and put a gun to his head. "Hold it right there," he said viciously.

Luke swung around and sneered at Balding, "You cops are always the same but my mate here ain't too keen on 'em."

"Why do you need to kill her?" demanded Balding, plucking up courage.

"Why? It's a deal that I made. Hah! What would you do if you were on a crippled plane hurtling towards the ground? I made a deal and then I did what was necessary to get out of there. There was a man on the plane who had smuggled a gun on board and he stood up and held us all prisoners. He was really just looking for one man, a guy called James. Some internet tycoon or something. When James stood up, the man let off several shots. Some hit their target, others hit other things. The plane took a dive and somehow I knew that it was going to crash, that the pilot could not regain control. That's when I heard the voice. It told me where to find an emergency' chute. With it on I opened an emergency exit and jumped clear."

"Wait! You're that famous guy who's supposed to have died in a plane crash," said Balding.

"Yes," answered Luke, "and, yet, here I am in the flesh and all I have to do now is pull this trigger and then I can get on with my life."

At that he turned his attention back to Jenny who still remained in his grip, "Say your prayers, little girl!" he sneered.

There was a sudden movement behind Luke and a strong arm grabbed him by the throat and threw him to the ground. Balding, at the same moment, took his chance, broke free from Jones' hold, wrestled him to the floor and knocked him out with a rock that he found nearby.

Luke had landed heavily on his back and could now see the man who had attacked him. Luke recognised the orange clothing and knew that it was the escaped convict and it struck terror into his heart. He was now bearing down on top of him. Silas locked his hands around Luke's throat and strangled the life out of him. Seeing this, Rob, the third man in the gang stepped backwards in fear. Silas and Balding soon turned their attention on him so he took bigger steps backwards, pointing his gun randomly at anyone and everyone. Suddenly, he tripped over a branch and fell backwards letting his gun go off aimlessly into the sky. Quickly, he scrambled back to his feet, dropped the gun and fled into the forest.

Jenny, now safe to move, hurried to where her uncle lay and began to cry. She knew that that some people would be likely to get hurt but she never thought that her uncle Val would be one of them. Harold and Suzie both came running and tried their best to comfort Jenny.

"Mummy! Your face!" Jenny said anxiously as she looked up at Suzie.

She was bleeding from her lips and nose having received a direct blow to the face from Luke.

"I'll be ok, darling," she said despite the pain, "I am just so happy that you are safe. Let's stand back and allow your daddy to say goodbye to his brother."

Jenny stood up and Suzie carried her away from Val and brought her over towards Silas but stopping about six feet away from him. She let Jenny back down on to her feet but Jenny held on to her tightly. They both stood and looked at the man who had saved them. He was rugged looking and dressed strangely in an orange jumpsuit. Then Balding came over.

"Thank you both," Suzie said expressing her gratitude, "what are your names?"

"Silas."

"I'm Balding."

"Thank you Silas and Balding, I don't know what would have happened if you hadn't stopped that awful man."

Jenny and Silas looked at each other and recognised each other from their dreams.

"That's the man who came to speak to me when I was on the swing," Jenny announced to Suzie.

Just then, another loud bang sounded from the edge of the forest. Jenny and Suzie watched with horror as Silas dropped to the ground, first to his knees, then on to his face. Jenny was confronted by a horror that reminded her of seeing her parents' dead bodies. Instinctively she stepped behind Suzie.

Two men came out from the forest with a woman walking out in front of them. It was Barbara followed by the pastor and the senator. Unaware, she had gone to the pastor to hand in her notice not knowing of his involvement in the plot to kill Jenny or the meeting that had happened at the house that night. She had said too much. The pastor had got talking to her and she accidentally mentioned she had to go to a meeting. The pastor had already figured out that, as he had caught her and the gardener praying that they could be fanatics. Once the pastor challenged Barbara, and she blurted out the truth, both he and the senator became very eager to attend the meeting. The senator had no fear and was well used to having to take care of things himself just like when his son almost ended up linked to a fanatic plot.

As soon as Johnson saw that his beloved Barbara was their prisoner, he made a dash for her.

"Stay right where you are!" instructed the senator sharply, aiming his gun at him.

Johnson halted reluctantly. The senator pushed Barbara on to her knees and held his gun to the back of her head.

"Bring out the girl, the little girl," he shouted, "If you don't I'll shoot this woman dead."

"Nooooo!" screamed Johnson in defiance.

"I'll give you three seconds," shouted the senator and began to count, "One!"

Johnson held his breath.

"Two!" shouted the senator.

No one moved. No one wanted to give the girl up.

"Three!"

"Wait!" cried Jenny as she came out from behind Suzie. Suzie immediately tried to move between her and the gun, but Jenny turned to her, "its okay, mummy," she announced sincerely, "it really is".

"What age are you little girl?" demanded the senator.

"I'm four," answered Jenny, looking directly at him.

"Huh! All this trouble over a four year old girl. Do you believe in God?"

She nodded.

"Goooood!" he said smirking, "then, why don't you close your eyes and say a prayer to him."

When Jenny closed her eyes to pray, the power of the Holy Spirit filled her.

The senator raised the gun and aimed it at her head, but was suddenly overcome by a presence which seemed strange to him. He could no longer move his finger to pull the trigger.

"Dear Father in heaven," Jenny said, praying in the power of the Holy Spirit, "if this bad man won't say sorry and go away, then I ask that you mind me and send your fire down to burn him up."

Then she opened her eyes and looked directly at the senator without a trace of fear.

The senator smirked. He was about to mock her when there was a sudden flash of light in the sky and an enormous bolt hit him in the chest. Looking down, he saw his clothes smouldering and inside a great hole had appeared in his chest. Breathless and overcome with shock, he collapsed to the ground in terrible agony. Immediately, his clothes burst into flames and he was soon engulfed. The pastor who had been standing next to the senator was now confronted by the eyes of the little four year old. He was totally at a loss, having seen God at work.

"I don't understand," he sobbed, repeating the words over and over. He was now a broken man.

"All you know is religion and greed but the Lord God Almighty sees the heart of a man and yours is as wicked as it gets. So God will come against you now. You shall watch as all that you love is taken away from you," declared Jenny, speaking prophetically to the pastor.

The pastor turned on his heels and began to run back toward his beloved mansion but, far above him, more meteorites were flying across the night sky and all of them were headed directly towards Hope. Some instantly hit his house, setting it on fire. Others began to pound other houses, businesses and public buildings right across town, causing many of them to catch fire.

With the pastor gone, Jenny and Balding, and a few others, gathered around where Silas had fallen. One of them rolled him over on to his back. He lay there staring up at them all and coughed up a little blood. Jenny's presence caught his attention and he turned his head to look at her.

"Are you the bad man that saw me on the swing?" she asked.

He nodded painfully.

"Are you sorry for all the bad things you have done?" she continued.

He nodded again, tears forming in his eyes. He feared that his time was up.

John came and knelt next to Jenny beside him.

"Jesus loves you! He died to pay for your sins so that you can be forgiven and come to know him," explained John, "He is the one who has been talking to you in your dreams and reminding you of all that you have done. He doesn't want to punish you but to draw you to him so that you will know him. Would you like to know Jesus like that?"

Silas nodded his head and began to pray, "I am sorry, Jesus. Please forgive me."

As he said the words, he saw a man in white appear before them all. His face shone brighter than anything he had ever seen before. He bent down and helped Silas to his feet and then hugged him tightly.

"I've waited all your life for you to come to me," he said, looking Silas in the eyes, "I have come so that you may live. Now, let us go and walk together."

Everyone saw Silas rise to his feet. They heard him talking to someone and perceived that it must be Jesus. They continued watching as Silas walked off into the forest, apparently healed of every wound.

Jenny stood there waving goodbye and just as Silas reached the forest, he turned his face towards her and she now saw that his face was shining. He waved and then stepped into the darkness of the forest with the Lord at his side. Jenny knew that she would see him again one day but not for many years to come.

John went over to a truck that was parked nearby and climbed up on to the back of it.

"Gather around, everyone," he called.

All the people came over to him and stood around the truck listening.

"Tonight has been a challenge. Tonight we say goodbye to our brother, Val, who now sits in heaven with our Lord. He has been called home but we must continue on here. We have seen God move this very night to defend his people. Two of the main instigators who were hounding Jenny are now removed from their places of authority. Now having seen God at work, are there any here who do not yet know Jesus?"

As he asked, several people moved to the front, including Sarah, Mr Balding, Linda and her children. So John took time to pray with each of them and to guide them in their first steps toward knowing Jesus. With each person you could notice an immediate change as he talked and prayed with them. They had not become more religious, nor did they have a life with less sin. The change was that they now walked with Jesus. Those who were already believers gathered around and welcomed each of them joyfully into the family with smiles and hugs.

Then John spoke to them all again.

"Are there any couples here who have come to dedicate their relationships and to be married before God? Are there people ready to declare this very night, that their relationships and future marriages belong to Him? Marriage is not an institution owned by the state. It is a wonderful thing that was given by God and belongs to God. Those of you who recognise God as sovereign and who wish to be married before Him, please step forward now."

Three couples stepped forwards: Sarah and Steve, Johnson and Barbara, Smith and Lisa. So right there, John quickly conducted a marriage ceremony as time was short. Then he instructed them to 'go forth and multiply'.

Finally, John dismissed all the people with final instructions, "Tell everyone you meet about what happened here tonight and why fire came down from the sky."

Smith and Lisa came up to John and thanked him for helping them to get their relationship right before God.

"Lisa," said John, "you know that, spiritually speaking, you marry any person who has been your lover. But, when this is not done before God, it is a perverted thing that twists the hearts of those involved. So, now, I pray this over you both that any wrongful spiritual ties in your lives be broken in Jesus name. Tonight you have lost a husband who was an ungodly man and who treated you harshly. He has now received his punishment, so in my heart I hope that you may go and sin no more. You both are now married so you must follow God in a godly way, lest he bring judgement to your door also. This will be a journey with much to learn, so if you keep your minds and hearts focused on God, then he will guide you and teach you."

With that, John reached into his pocket and pulled out a small Bible. Handing it to them, he said with a warm smile, "Take this, read it and continue to seek God together and he will teach you all you need to know and do."

"I think I have something here for you," stated Smith.

He removed the rucksack from his back and handed it to John.

John opened the rucksack, looked inside and smiled, "Everything is as I had prayed," he said.

The people who knew Val wanted to stay behind for his burial and a group of them helped to dig a grave and to lower him carefully into the ground. Harold, Suzie and Jenny were very upset but they said their goodbyes and understood that he was now in a better place and that they would see him again.

After that, on instructions from John, they took the bodies of the others who had died, the senator and Luke and placed them in the cabin. Immediately, fire fell from the sky and the cabin was incinerated in minutes. After that, the majority of the crowd dispersed. 'HSP' was at an end.

John, Sarah and Steve, Harold, Suzie and Jenny gathered together to say their farewell.

"Where will you go now, John?" asked Sarah.

"A man who follows God is like the wind," he replied, "there is no telling which way it will blow, only that it will surely blow. What about you two?"

She answered, smiling "I think, we will get used to being married and settle in this area for a while. I still have so much to learn from Steve about God."

John nodded.

"I like what you said," said Harold, "but I don't quite know what to do next. We had been depending heavily on Val for the steps that brought us here and now he is gone. Regarding what you said about the wind, how does that work? How do we do that now?" he asked, his arms around both Suzie and Jenny.

"It's all to do with faith," said John, "trust in God, Harold. He will guide each of you, and guide each of you safely."

Most of the people who had come to the 'HSP' returned calmly to their homes and found that their property remained undamaged from the meteorites. However, they noticed that people who had failed to come to the meeting had suffered at least some damage to their homes. So the believers went and spread the good news, explaining to their neighbours what had taken place that night. Some people saw it merely as a nice story. Others were touched by the Holy Spirit and repented of the sinful lives that they had lived. Because of this, the number of believers in the area increased rapidly.

Michelle was driving through the night but realised that she would soon need another top-up of fuel, so she turned off to look for gas at a nearby town called Hope. As she got nearer, she was astounded to find many of the houses on fire. She stopped her car immediately, not believing her eyes.

As she got out of the car, she started to realise that this was too good a story to miss out on. She asked a teenage boy who was nearby to be her cameraman and quickly showed him the basic workings of her camera. Then the two of them went from house to house looking for a good story. Eventually she found a man who would talk to her.

"This is Michelle of Channel Seven News. I am here in the town of Hope where, it seems several buildings are on fire. Can you tell me, sir, what happened here tonight?"

"It was a miracle," the man declared, "look around you. Do you see anyone putting out the flames?"

The boy swung around with the camera and saw that what the man said was true. Everyone was standing clear of the flames but no hoses or buckets of water were being used to quench the flames. They were letting the houses burn to the ground.

"Is that your house?" asked Michelle.

"It was," said the man, "I had the best of everything, a fifty-inch TV, a brand new leather suite and the most comfortable bed in town. I had everything but it's all gone now."

"I'm sorry," said Michelle, trying to show feeling for his loss.

"Don't be sorry," the man chuckled, "tonight I have come to understand the truth – that everything that I had spent my life gathering was nothing in comparison to the hope of knowing Jesus. God has sent fire from the heavens to burn up our homes because we loved these material things too much. God has corrected us."

When the man had said this, he fell to his knees, beginning to sob and cry out, "I've wasted my life, Lord. Take what is left! My life is now yours!"

Michelle backed away and signalled for the young man to stop recording. Then she led him along the street to find other people to speak to. Everyone that they met shared similar stories and she became quite frustrated. Finally, she saw a man running through the streets whom she recognised. She stepped out and stopped him.

"Pastor, can you tell me what has taken place here tonight?"

She was astounded as he said, "It is all foolishness, our religions, our traditions and our global agreements. Tonight, God has humbled me. Inside, I feel like Judas on the day when he handed Jesus over to be arrested. If any of my congregation happens to be watching this, I want to say that I am sorry for the lies I told you. You were deceived but now I exhort you to turn to Jesus."

He hobbled off having said all he could. Michelle noted the torment that was evident in his eyes.

Although Michelle did not fully understand what had taken place there that night, she did understand that she was meant to find it just as it was and report on it.

The news got out that Luke was still alive but that news became overshadowed by the story of a pastor who had suddenly denounced the global church as being an organisation filled with deceivers. To quash the story, the video that Michelle brought back was soon discredited by the authorities who made a public statement that it was the fanatics who had burnt the town to the ground. They sent troops to the area to suppress any 'false beliefs'. However their actions had the exact opposite effect. Each of the soldiers who were sent became believers and, when they returned to where they had come from, the good news spread even faster. The video footage recorded that night went viral and was seen by people in every part of the globe. God had appeared and made himself known. Behind the scenes, the number of couples grew in numbers who no longer complied with the demands of the state. Instead, they now gave priority to what God required of them in order to live their lives in a way that pleased Him.

OTHER BOOKS BY THE AUTHOR

Prayers, Poems Songs

Book of Prophecies

Boy who Dreams

Be Revived *Prophecies & Revelations*

Be Revived *Open the Box*

Revival Prayers

Edify *Dreams Prophecies & Visions*

Faith Beyond Miracles

Calling the Bride Calling the Church

In Spirit and Truth

Prayers Prophecies Dreams

Made in the USA
Charleston, SC
19 October 2015